Full Count

The Paper Journey Press: http://the paper journey.com
First trade paperback edition
Manufactured in the United States of America

Library of Congress Control Number: 2005902983

International Standard Book Number (ISBN) 0970172664

full count

by Win Neagle

The Paper Journey Press
Wake Forest, NC

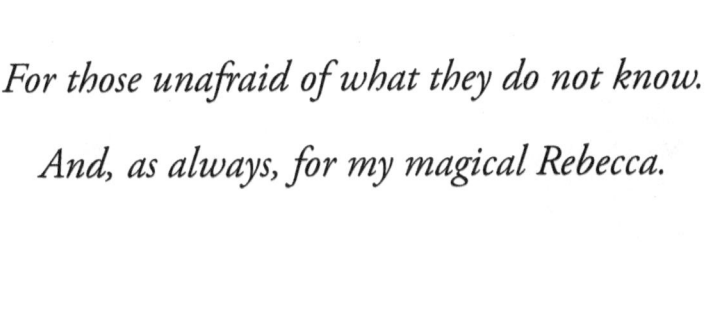

For those unafraid of what they do not know.

And, as always, for my magical Rebecca.

Full Count

full count

by Win Neagle

Batter Up

Billy Overby enters the batter's box just as he has every trip to the plate for the past two decades. He takes a deep breath, exhales, and places his right foot inside. Another inhalation brings the bat to Billy's shoulder, and a third breath ushers Billy's left foot into the box. As his left foot makes contact with the red dirt, Billy's gray eyes bulge slightly in concentration as he awaits the next pitch.

A Tarot card reader in Nashville believes that Billy's eye bulges are capable of sucking energy from opposing pitchers, while a yoga teacher in Minneapolis explains to her six-year-old son that it is a stress-relieving technique often practiced by Buddhist monks at the beginning of meditation. However, when a Kansas City sportswriter inquired about the bulges, Billy seemed to be sincerely unaware of the habit.

The nation has become obsessed with Billy's batting average. Conversations at barbershops, church dinners, construction sites, and playgrounds begin with speculations over whether he will become the first player since Ted Williams in 1941 to bat .400 in a single season.

High in the uppermost row of the outfield bleachers, twenty-year-old Ryan Rigsby sets his hot dog on the King James Bible resting in his lap, then trains his binoculars on Billy. Ryan believes if Overby bats over .400 for the season it will be a sign from God that the end of the world is near. "BELOVED, NOW WE ARE THE SONS OF GOD, AND IT DOTH NOT YET APPEAR WHAT WE SHALL BE, BUT WE KNOW THAT, WHEN HE SHALL APPEAR, WE SHALL BE LIKE HIM!" Ryan exclaims to no one in particular.

Full Count

Opening Pitch

As of this moment, Billy Overby has never fallen in love. Despite the fact he has enjoyed lots of sex with women of many different ages and physiques, outdoors and indoors, afternoon quickies and steamy all-nighters, the only thing akin to love to ever become passionately lodged in twenty-six-year old Billy Overby's soul is baseball.

Freud tells us that we have few conscious memories before the age of four, so as far as Billy knows, there was never a time when he wasn't attached to baseball. By Billy's fourth year, his father had taught him to swing a bat — a sawed-off pool stick with the tapered end wrapped in duct tape — from both sides of the plate. And then his father died.

Billy's earliest memories are of his grief-stricken mother pitching in relief.

There were years of financial hardship, and there are touching stories we could explore about the young boy having to be the man of the house, working odd jobs after practice and making home repairs while his schoolmates worried about little more than video game villains and history tests; but those days have passed, and now Billy's mother watches her son on a forty-two inch screen in the corner of the Billy Overby Foundation Soup Kitchen. She and her small staff watch along with more than a hundred of Raleigh's homeless to see if Billy will reach base against Colorado's prize starter, Clarence Macy. Thanks to Billy's prowess at the plate, the Carolina Waves, in only their third year of existence, find themselves two games behind first-place Colorado. More importantly, if Billy can get a hit off of Macy during this at bat, his average will rise to over .400 for the season.

This is the sixteenth time Clarence Macy has faced Billy Overby this season. The previous encounters have resulted in three walks, one strikeout, and a dismaying twelve hits. In an attempt to change his luck, Clarence has dedicated Overby's first at-bat to his fiancée and promised her a strikeout. This vow darts through Clarence's mind as he shakes his head at his catcher, Russ Mitchell, who is signaling for a curve ball. Thus far, Overby has never swung at one of Clarence's first pitches, so it seems appropriate to Clarence to hurl a fastball across the meat of the plate to go ahead in the count, but Russ Mitchell refuses to withdraw the curveball sign. Clarence shakes his head again, and Russ Mitchell capitulates, flicking his forefinger toward the ground to signal the fastball which Clarence launches at 94 miles per hour.

At this speed, it takes the baseball just over four-tenths of a second to reach home plate. Had Billy Overby had any intention of trying to hit this particular pitch, he would have had about half this time, approximately two-tenths of a second, to decide whether or not to swing. However, as Macy had guessed, Billy never intended to swing at this pitch, using it simply as an opportunity to take a clear look at what he can expect for the rest of the evening.

As the ball speeds past him, Billy detects a bit more heat on Macy's fastball than he recalls from their last meeting. The extra speed might be accounted for by Macy's vow to his leggy, caramel-skinned fiancée, Diane Duncan, who is in the seventh row behind the Colorado dugout telling herself that she will let the outcome of this at-bat decide whether or not she should listen to her mother, who tells her on a regular basis that she's out of her mind to be involved with a professional athlete and needs to patch things up with her ex who owns a chain of oyster bars along the East Coast and still sends flowers to Diane's mother on holidays.

As the fastball slaps into Russ Mitchell's mitt, the umpire deems it just high of the strike zone and Diane's mother goes ahead in the count: one ball, no strikes.

Two pitches later, Clarence Macy finds himself even further behind. How could I miss with three straight fastballs, he asks himself as he meets Russ Mitchell halfway between home plate and the pitcher's mound.

"Look, don't sweat it," Mitchell says, slapping the ball into Clarence's mitt. "Give him a curve, low and away. If you walk him, then we'll just get Grissom. He's only two for his last fifteen."

"No way. Overby never swings at 3-0 pitches. I'm bringing the heat."

Macy lifts his left leg and coils his body tight, storing the energy necessary to deliver a Major League fastball. As the ball leaves Macy's hand, Billy takes a stride in Macy's direction and his hips begin to open to the pitch. A split second later, his hips pull his arms around, which, in turn, signal his wrists to unleash his 31-ounce bat. Even before bat meets ball, Clarence Macy realizes that he should have listened to Russ Mitchell.

Billy's bat misses the center of the baseball by a quarter of an inch. This is just enough imperfection to launch the ball at a 45-degree trajectory high into the left field stands where it is pounced upon by a dozen youths from the Raleigh Children's Home.

Billy Overby circles the bases with the joy of a four-year-old sending a ball over the head of a man who loves him.

Diane Duncan speed dials the oyster bar mogul on her cell phone.

Ryan Rigsby lifts his Bible over his head, more convinced than ever that the end is near.

. . . . . .

On his sailboat a half mile off the North Carolina coast, Cameron Lawrence's radio batteries begin to die. As Macy steps into the windup of his next pitch, the voice of Waves announcer Hank Marrow turns to pure static.

"That's no good."

Cameron's girlfriend, Amanda, puts down her book. "What's wrong, honey?"

"I'm losing the game."

"That's no problem. I have a game I promise you won't lose," says Amanda, attempting to tug Cameron over to her side of the sea-dampened mattress.

"Not now. After the game." Cameron steps into the galley, opens its lone drawer, and removes extra batteries from a Ziploc bag.

"How did this happen? Not only am I in a relationship with a gay man, but I get the only gay man in America obsessed with baseball," Amanda says from behind her book.

"Given that we've been going out for over a year now, don't you think it's about time you stopped thinking of me as gay?"

"And after a year, I find myself in the middle of the ocean, lonely on a soggy mattress, while you fantasize about a bunch of men in tight little uniforms."

Cameron pretends to ignore the remark in order to focus on the battery transplant. By the time Hank Marrow's voice is resurrected, the inning has just ended and the station takes a commercial break.

As Billy trots onto the diamond, he takes time to survey the bright lights against the night sky. He surveys the stands. He can never get used to the idea that thousands of fans pay to watch men play this children's game. With the tip of

 *Full Count*

his hat he gives silent thanks to all of them.

"Please don't," Cameron says calmly. Amanda has removed herself from the damp bed to yank the radio from the table. As she makes her way onto the deck, Cameron once again asks her to reconsider. "Really. Please don't."

But once she makes a decision, Amanda stays the course. It is this doggedness that has made her one of the top real estate agents in the Raleigh area. It is this same doggedness that sends Cameron's radio out into the night sky and eventually to a barnacled retirement on the ocean floor.

"I wish you wouldn't have done that," Cameron says, leaning over the boat's low railing to scan the black water.

"I know that, Cameron. If you had wanted me to do it, it wouldn't have been necessary." Amanda pulls a lighter and a pack of cigarettes from her shirt pocket.

"Can I have one?"

As Cameron and Amanda smoke in silence, the lapping of water against the boat is all that distracts them from the truth that has become more and more obvious: their relationship is ending.

By the time Macy is pulled from the game in the sixth inning, Billy Overby has tallied two more hits. Even though Billy lines out to third in the eighth inning against Colorado reliever Tricks McGraw, he finishes the game batting .402, having hit safely 212 times in 528 at-bats.

"I really care about you. You know that, right?" Cameron says, reaching for Amanda's hand in the dark, but knocking his knuckles against a cleat instead.

"Then how can you insist on living on this sad little

boat? I can't do this any more, Cameron. I need you in Raleigh."

For the past fifteen months, Cameron and Amanda's relationship has subsisted on weekend sailing jaunts supplemented by a spattering of inland visits by Cameron.

"Raleigh suffocates me. You know I need the water."

Cameron has lived on *Sam I Am* for almost four years. His main source of income is the sale of his oil seascapes. Presently there are twenty-seven paintings of various shades of blue and green hanging on the walls of Amanda's house, hoping to fetch the four to six hundred dollars asked by their price tags.

"Maybe it's the idea of being around me all the time that suffocates you," Amanda suggests.

"Maybe." He had meant to say it sarcastically, but somewhere between conception and utterance Cameron realized Amanda was right. He is about to apologize when Amanda begins punching his shoulder.

"I hate you. I hate you. I hate you," Amanda chants in rhythm with her punches. But she does not hate Cameron any more than she hates herself for falling into a situation which never had a chance of ending in anything other than heartache. She knows it has nothing to do with Cameron's nebulous sexual orientation—girlfriends nearly as plentiful as boyfriends in his past—for their sex life has not declined appreciably since their first night of lovemaking when Cameron found himself docked at the same Charleston marina where Amanda and a dozen old college girlfriends were basing their houseboat reunion.

The first thing Cameron said to Amanda when she invited herself onto his boat was, "You need to know that this is going to hurt one of us."

But by then it was too late. She had already climbed into his smell.

 *Full Count*

Billy Overby has been doused in beer by his teammates, showered, and been doused in beer again. His mood is dampened only slightly when Waves pitcher Mark Crocker steps between the sea of reporters to speak to him. "Billy, we're still on for fishing tomorrow, right?"

Billy had forgotten that three weeks ago he accepted Crocker's invitation to go deep sea fishing on one of the month's three off days. Billy has little interest in fishing, but he tells himself it might offer a reprieve from the onslaught of the media, which grows more and more intense as the end of the season gets closer. Judging from the frenzy in the locker room, breaking the four hundred mark is going to make things even worse. "Sure, count me in."

It is well past midnight. Cameron's deep breathing seems to be in perfect cadence with the gentle rise and fall of the ocean, but while Amanda finds the rhythm relaxing, she cannot sleep. She is thinking of the week she and Cameron spent on Shackleford Banks and how the island's wild horses approached Cameron like a long lost friend. She is thinking of the first storm she weathered on *Sam I Am* and how Cameron had gone on deck to shout Whitman verses into the howling wind. She is thinking of the first drawing he ever did of her and how she cried because with just a few simple lines he had proven that he saw her more clearly than anyone else ever had.

But more than anything, she thinks of his smell. Whether he was fist deep in the guts of fish or saturated in the sweat of their lovemaking, whether he was inhaling cigarettes or gulping gin, nothing could ever extinguish the intoxicating smell that was his and his alone, a mixture of meadow and mud, or vinegar and honey, or maybe one part honeysuckle and two parts blood. More than anything, she will miss his smell.

For the rest of her life, she will both love and hate him for his captivating smell.

When Billy's alarm goes off at three a.m., his mouth is parched and his head is swollen from champagne and gin. The idea of a three-hour drive to go deep-sea fishing, which only several hours earlier had seemed like a perfect adventure, now has the tint of self-imposed torture.

Billy rolls over and dials up Mark Crocker with the hope that Mark might have had a similar change of heart, but he is met with the news that Mark and Wave's second-baseman Gary Ashton have already loaded Mark's Suburban and will be in Billy's driveway within minutes.

"Come on, the fish are waiting," Mark calls from the driver's window as Billy stumbles half awake down his drive.

When Billy opens the rear door of the Suburban, a young woman thrusts a bourbon bottle at him. Billy declines. "No, thanks, I make it a rule not to drink before sunrise."

The woman shrugs and hands the bottle to Gary, who takes a quick slug and passes the bottle to a copper-skinned woman in the passenger seat whose pearly teeth offer a pleasant smile as Mark offers introductions. "Sky and Amber, meet the best goddamned hitter of the twenty-first century. Billy, meet the best goddamned strippers on the east coast."

Billy is not the least surprised by the additional guests. Mark Crocker runs on liquor and women. He once told Billy that the world and its inhabitants are no different than an orange being swarmed by ants, and that people have every reason to be depressed by the chaos, but personally, he's going to enjoy all the orange he can cram in his mouth.

It turns out that Sky and Amber aren't so bad at cramming things into their mouths, either. By the time the Suburban pulls into the Sunrise Marina where Mark Crocker moors *Screwball III*, his fifty-five foot fishing yacht, Sky and Amber have orally pleased not only their fishing escorts, but also the young trooper who pulled Crocker as he was driving a hundred and twenty miles per hour with Amber wedged beneath the dash.

Within minutes of arriving at the marina, the crew is ready to set out. Billy and Gary have transferred five buckets of fried chicken and two gallons of bourbon from the Suburban to the yacht's galley; Amber and Sky have removed skimpy jean shorts to reveal even skimpier bikinis as they unfurl beach towels on the bow; and Mark has climbed up nine rungs to the cockpit without spilling a drop of his cocktail. Unfortunately, when Mark turns the key to crank up *Screwball III's* eight hundred and seventy-five horses of power, he is met with silence.

After a half hour of profanity and wire fiddling, *Screwball III* remains docked.

"He has a bit of a temper, doesn't he?" Sky says, nodding up to the cockpit.

"I guess that's fair to say," Billy replies.

"Not you. You're cool as a cucumber. I heard one of the announcers saying that the other night."

"They have to say something."

"Some people say you're the best there's ever been. Is that true?" Sky asks with a flirting smile.

Billy's discomfort grows. Amber and Gary are already below deck passing the maintenance time in one of the yacht's two cabins; but at present, Billy has no desire to inject Sky with any more of his bodily fluids. "Anyone who says I'm the best there's ever been is either a fool or my mother. I'm having a good season, and that's all anyone can say at this point."

Sensing Billy's irritation, Sky changes the subject. "A college kid told me the other night that I have the best tits he's ever seen," Sky says with a laugh.

"How long have you been dancing?"

"About five years."

"You like it?"

"It's been good to me. I got married at seventeen to a thirty-year-old asshole who beat me."

"Why'd you marry him?"

"He was rich and good looking. Very handsome. He didn't start beating me until a few months after we were married. One night he was knocking me around the kitchen, harder than usual. I was bleeding. I wasn't sure from where, but there was blood all over the linoleum. He came at me with his hand raised and I stuck a butcher knife in his ribs. I started dancing the next night and made enough money I didn't have to go back. Dancing might have saved my life."

"Did he die?"

"Hell, no. He was too mean to die... Would you mind putting some lotion on my back?" Sky rolls onto her belly and Billy squirts a line of lotion down her back. As he smears the line across Sky's shoulders, he tries to imagine what it must be like to be so small. Sky's shoulders are not much wider than the span between Billy's thumb and pinky, and he imagines her cowering, trapped in a kitchen as her drunk husband moves in for another blow. Billy tries to imagine feeling as physically vulnerable as Sky must have felt as she grasped the butcher knife.

"Can I ask you a question, Sky?"

"Keep rubbing and ask away."

"Do you want to be here?"

"Of course...Look, Mr. Big Bat, I don't do anything I

don't want to."

"But would you want to be here if Crocker wasn't paying you?"

Sky lets out a sigh of contentment as Billy kneads her shoulders. "Yeah, I think I would, but don't tell your buddy. He's one of my best customers."

Billy is about to promise not to leak any of Sky's business information when the shouting from a nearby sailboat distracts him.

In the spring of 1957, Bob Riesener was standing on the edge of a life-long dream. As a pitcher for the Class C minor league Alexandria Stallions, Riesener felt that all that separated him from the major leagues was one solid season on the mound.

From the very start it was obvious that 1957 was Riesener's year, and after five months of bus rides from one cheap motel, greasy diner, and hostile minor league ballpark to the next, Riesener had compiled an immaculate record of twenty-one wins and no losses, proving himself to be the top minor league pitcher in the nation.

But Riesener's dream of moving on to the big leagues was not to be realized. Had the Alexandria Stallions been connected with any team other than the New York Yankees, Riesener would have spent the following season in the first class hotels and charter planes of the big leagues, but because the Yankees' line-up already featured one of the strongest pitching staffs in baseball history, Riesener remained a Stallion.

He would end his career without ever stepping foot on a major league field.

Amanda knows how Bob Riesener must have felt.

As Cameron negotiates the channel into the Sunrise Marina, she sits wrapped in a towel, contemplating the state of her relationship with Cameron. For the past fifteen months she has been the perfect mate. She has nurtured

Cameron's body, mind, and soul. She has accepted Cameron for who he is—a somewhat adolescent male who refuses to accept that there can be more to life on land than a job, a house, and a lifetime of debt—and she has never asked him to be anything else. She has embraced his art, his boat, and his idea that he can be fully committed to a relationship without leaving the water. But now she wants more, and she knows she is not going to get it. Amanda says goodbye to the fantasies she has nurtured while showing houses to other couples. She and Cameron will never share a ranch house in Apex, or a colonial in North Raleigh, or even a townhouse in Wake Forest. Looking back, Amanda tells herself she should have known from the very beginning.

After Amanda's first night with Cameron, she knew she needed more of him. Back at the houseboat she told her friends of Cameron's smell and of his skills as a lover, and her friends convinced her to do what she already knew she would do: Amanda phoned her office to cancel her appointments and arranged for her partner to cover the two closings she had scheduled for the week.

She was going to spend the next seven days with a stranger in the middle of the ocean. She could not have been more frightened or exhilarated.

When Amanda returned to Cameron's boat with her packed bag and two burgers from the marina's grill, he welcomed her aboard, but his eyes gave away a bit of surprise.

"You were serious about the offer, weren't you?" she asked as Cameron tossed her bag below deck.

"Of course. I just didn't think you'd accept."

"Do none of the other women accept?"

"It's not like that. I've never really offered before...It's just that this is a pretty small boat, and I'm not always the best with company."

Amanda was beginning to get cold feet, but before she could consider disembarking, a slight breeze ushered a full sniff of Cameron into her nostrils. Her knees quivered and her heart thwacked against her sternum. "Then you'll just have to teach me to sail, so I can throw you overboard if things get too cramped."

"It's a deal. Let's eat those burgers." Cameron disappeared briefly below deck and returned with two metal plates, a bag of chips, and a bottle of chardonnay.

Following lunch, Cameron and Amanda left port, sailing north. For the next six hours Amanda studied Cameron as he performed the dance of sailing, moving around the deck from one line to another as he explained jibes and tacks, the art of trimming the main sail and jib, the difference between a reach and a run, the riggings of a sloop versus a cutter, and how to read thunderheads and squall lines, neither of which were anywhere in sight. For all the information Cameron barked out during Amanda's first day of sailing, she was relatively certain of only two things: starboard referred to the right side of the boat and Cameron Lawrence was one of the sexiest, most intriguing men she had ever known.

As dusk approached, Cameron added fishing to his other tasks. He baited a line with two minnows from a well in the deck and cast the line off the back of the boat. Within minutes he reeled the line in and plucked the hook from the mouth of a six-inch fish.

"Pinfish," Cameron announced, holding the fish up for Amanda's inspection.

"I'm very impressed, but if that's dinner, I hope you're not too hungry."

Cameron laughed and placed the fish on a different piece of tackle, this one with a much larger hook, which he attached to the line and cast back into the water. "Now it's your turn. Hold this."

"I can't. I've never fished before."

Cameron laughed again and positioned Amanda's hands on the reel. "The only thing you can do wrong is let go."

"But I have been known to let go."

As Cameron folded the small sail on the front of the mast, he quizzed Amanda. "What's this sail called?"

Amanda thought it might be a jib, but before she could offer her guess, the fishing rod tried to leap out of her hands. Overcompensating, she fell backwards onto the deck, her left hip taking the brunt of the fall as her hands remained firmly clamped on the rod and reel.

"Are you okay?" Cameron called from the bow, his arms filled with sail.

"I think so. What do I do?" Amanda asked, suddenly aware that a living creature —a fairly large living creature from the feel of things—was now connected to her via a stretch of fishing line. "Should I stand up?"

"No. Stay on the deck. Try to crank the reel clockwise."

Amanda's arms were well conditioned thanks to her tri-weekly, hour-long workouts at the gym, but even straining with all she had, she could not budge the reel. "I can't."

Cameron's excitement grew. "That's great. It looks like we'll have enough for dinner, after all."

Cameron wrapped a line around the jib—maybe it was the adrenaline pumping through Amanda's body, but it occurred to her that she was now certain that the smaller sail was called the jib—and hurried across the deck. He sat behind her, his arms reaching around her so that he could place his hands on top of hers.

Cameron leaned back, pulling the rod and Amanda with him. As he guided their torsos forward again, Cameron led Amanda's right hand in quick circles, reeling in the

slack they had gained. This was the only lesson Amanda needed. Surrounded by a musky cloud of Cameron's scent, Amanda used her abdomen and lower back to pull the rod against the line's resistance, and then quickly reeled in as she leaned forward. Rocking and reeling in, rocking and reeling in, Amanda felt the sea creature grow closer.

Several minutes into the struggle, Amanda saw a silvery shadow just below the water's surface. Cameron rose, grabbed the line in his hand, and pulled the fish out of the water and onto the deck. "It's an albacore. One of the biggest I've seen."

As the fish gasped for life, Amanda felt a mixture of grief and elation. She could feel her pulse in the fatigued muscles of her back and arms, and an impressive bruise was already forming on her backside, but she felt great, one hundred percent alive. Cameron struck the fish in the head with the handle of a long, curved knife, but the fish continued to flap its gills against the air. Cameron struck the fish again and its struggle ceased.

After he had secured the main sail and set the anchor, Cameron headed and gutted the fish and cut it into four large steaks which he doused in lemon juice and grilled on a hibachi attached to the boat's railing. He wrapped a half dozen new potatoes in metal foil and dropped them directly onto the coals. Then he opened another bottle of wine, and by the time Amanda had finished her first plastic cupful, dinner was ready.

"You're quite the chef," said Amanda.

"There wouldn't have been anything to cook if you weren't quite the fisherman, so cheers to both of us," Cameron toasted.

"Yes, to us, whoever we are."

Cameron filled Amanda's cup. "Who are we?" he asked.

"I don't know. Strangers, I guess."

Cameron took a sip of wine and slowly chewed a bite of fish.

"Do you really think we're strangers?" Cameron asked, taking another sip of wine and looking directly into Amanda's eyes.

"Technically speaking, yes. Technically speaking, we are two strangers who had sex last night and are now dining on a fish I caught with your help."

"Doesn't that at least make us fishing buddies?"

Amanda laughed. "I guess you're right. We're fishing buddies."

"Can I ask one more question?"

"Go ahead."

"What's the best way to let one's fishing buddy know that you'd like the two of you to get real close and naked?"

"I'm not sure. Maybe after dinner you can show me around below deck and see if you can figure it out."

But Cameron and Amanda never made it below deck. After dinner, Cameron asked Amanda if he might steal a kiss, and by the time their bodies separated, the sky was full of stars.

After a swim in the warm, black water, a quick freshwater rinse, and a short nap below deck, Cameron and Amanda donned shorts and sweaters, opened another bottle of wine, and sat on deck, Amanda leaning into Cameron who leaned back against the mast.

"So how long have you lived on this boat?" Amanda asked, mostly just to hear Cameron's voice.

"About three years now."

"That's a long time."

"I guess so."

"What do you do for entertainment?"

"Have you not been properly entertained?"

Amanda gave Cameron a playful elbow to his ribs. "I mean when you're alone. Doesn't it get boring sometimes, out here all by yourself?"

"Not really. There's usually a pretty good movie showing."

"Oh, really? What's playing tonight?"

Cameron scanned the sky. "Let's see, it looks like the curtain might be going up on Perseus Two," Cameron said, pointing to a cluster of stars just above the horizon.

"Kind of pretty. But doesn't appear to have much of a plot."

"Oh, you're kidding, right? There's not a better story around."

"Tell me about Perseus Two, then," Amanda said, snuggling her shoulders further into Cameron and inhaling his aroma, which brought to mind the image of steaks grilling outside in the cold. A hint of ginger trickled in. And maybe the faintest trace of garlic.

"Where should we start? Before we get into the sequel, there are some things you need to know about the original. You didn't see Perseus One, did you?"

"I'm afraid I missed it."

"You should see it if you get the chance. In the original Perseus, we meet King Acrisius of Argos who is distraught over his lack of a male heir. Not knowing what else to do, he makes an appointment with his oracle who informs him that no heirs are on the horizon."

"Poor King Acrisius."

"It gets worse. Not only will he have no heirs, but he learns that his daughter, Dana, will give birth to a grandson who is destined to kill him, so he imprisons Dana in an underground vault to keep her safe from impregnation."

"What other choice would a brave father have?"

"He did give her a skylight."

"What a generous soul."

"Did I mention that Dana is absolutely beautiful?"

"As beautiful as me?"

"Almost."

"But I bet she never caught a fish."

"I'm not so sure, because Zeus spies Dana in her bronze dungeon—"

"You didn't say it was bronze."

"It's bronze. With a skylight."

"That's a little better, then."

"Except that the skylight allows Zeus to take the form of a golden rainfall and wash down upon Dana. Nine months later she gives birth."

"To Perseus?"

"Exactly."

"That must have shaken old Acrisius."

"It certainly did, but once again, Acrisius proves to be the compassionate father. Rather than putting his daughter and grandson to death, he merely puts them in a chest and throws them into the ocean."

"And that's when Dana may have caught a fish."

"Maybe."

"I bet she didn't."

"We'll say she didn't."

"Thanks."

"So after being adrift for many days without catching a fish, the chest eventually washes ashore on a small island where Dana and young Perseus are discovered by Dictys, a kindly, old fisherman who takes Dana and Perseus home. After a short discussion, Dictys and Mrs. Dictys decide to look after Dana and treat Perseus as the son they never had."

"A happy ending."

"Yes. For Perseus One, at least."

Amanda clapped.

 *Full Count*

"But there's more," Cameron said.

"Perseus Two?"

"Yes. Right away Dana's beauty stirs up more trouble."

" But she still hasn't ever caught a fish."

"No, but Dictys's brother, the evil tyrant King Polydectes, becomes smitten with the beautiful Dana who has never caught a fish."

"This isn't a very believable story. Why would anyone be smitten with someone who has never caught a fish?"

"You're right. Maybe Dictys teaches Dana how to fish."

"No, no, no. Dana never catches a fish. The evil king just has bad taste."

"That's it. Polydectes, the evil king with bad taste, falls for Dana and sees Perseus as a hindrance to his courtship, so what he does, and this is the only part of the movie the critics didn't care for, he marries another woman so that everyone will have to bring a gift to the reception. But he knows Perseus won't be able to bring a gift and instead will end up making some foolish promise, like vowing to bring Polydectes and his new wife the head of Medusa."

"I think the critics have a legitimate gripe."

"Nevertheless, Perseus is now obligated to secure Medusa's head, the sight of which has turned countless men to stone."

"Perseus has been through a lot in his young life. I think he's up for the challenge," Amanda said, turning to put her cheek against Cameron's chest, thus gaining a better olfactory vantage point. She smelled sweat-covered rose petals, evoking an image of a perspiring rickshaw driver running through a Tokyo herb market. "Did you know that the rickshaw was invented by a Baptist missionary?"

Cameron was not fazed by the non sequitur. "I can't think of a better way for neophytes in Christ to prove their devotion to their selfless converters."

"Are you religious?"

"Never had the legs for it."

"Me neither. Tell me more about our poor Perseus."

"The first problem is that Perseus has no idea where to find Medusa and her Gorgon sisters, so he goes to see an oracle in Delphi who sends him to Dodona, the land of whispering oaks."

"Do the oaks know where Medusa is?"

"Do you always talk this much during a movie?"

"Only if I like the movie," Amanda said, kissing Cameron's chin.

"The oaks have no idea where Medusa is, but just as Perseus is regretting his vow to Polydectes, Hermes shows up and leads Perseus to the Stygian nymphs who give Perseus a pair of flying sandals, a magic satchel, and a helmet of invisibility."

Amanda wrapped her arms around Cameron and breathed deeply. "What's a Stygian nymph?"

"I'm not really sure, but Perseus appreciates their generosity, and with some coaching from Hermes and Athena—"

"When did Athena show up?" Amanda asked. She inhaled and felt her muscles relax completely as Cameron's scent wrapped around her brain, filling it with images of lemon trees, rainy mornings, and campfires. Before Cameron could finish the story—Perseus's eventual victory over Medusa and Polydectes's being turned to stone—she was asleep.

As Cameron carried Amanda below deck to put her in bed, she mumbled softly, "What about Acrisius?"

"He went into hiding on the island of Larissa. Then one day he was watching an athletic competition when the wind blew a discus into the crowd. It struck Acrisius in the head and killed him," Cameron explained as he laid

 *Full Count*

Amanda gently on the bed.

"Perseus?"

"Yes, Perseus was the discus thrower."

And with that, Amanda fell into a deep sleep which was filled with pleasant dreams interrupted only briefly by the image of Acrisius lying on the deck of the boat, a fishing line in his mouth, and Cameron striking him repeatedly with a discus.

What Amanda sees now that she hadn't seen during that first week with Cameron is that the other woman had been right there under her nose from the start. In the beginning, the boat had been a stage, a convenient setting for sunrises, skinny dips, and nightly stories beneath the stars; but now Amanda sees *Sam I Am* for what she is, the owner of Cameron's heart. Worse than the most abominable mother-in-law or seductive mistress, the boat is the one thing that stands between Amanda and happiness, and she has listened to enough Greek mythology during the past fifteen months to know that there is only one cure for a formula such as the one she finds herself in. Someone must die.

Mark Crocker is about to give up on starting *Screwball III* when he slams a frustrated fist into the console. The vibrations of the punch appear to straighten out the misbehaving electrical system, and with a turn of the key, the boat's twin motors gurgle loudly. "Let's launch, fellows. Untie the bow line, will you, Billy?"

Billy is a bit disappointed. He and Sky have enjoyed eavesdropping on the lovers' quarrel two boats down.

"He's being asinine," says Sky.

"What's he done? He's been honest all along."

"No, he hasn't. Telling the truth and being honest are two totally different things."

Billy wants to hear more about the distinctions between truth and honesty, but before he can ask, the woman from the quarrel leaps onto the dock and stomps past *Screwball III*. Sky follows her.

Cameron has a pain deep in his gut. He wants Amanda to be happy, and he knows that he can't offer her the relationship she needs. As he watches Amanda march towards her car, he wonders what she is saying to the bikinied woman who has followed her.

He meant what he told Amanda last night. He loves her and, other than give up life on his sailboat, there is not much he wouldn't do for her.

"Girl, you just have to cut him loose," Sky says, as Amanda opens the passenger door to her Mercedes sedan and reaches beneath the seat.

"Oh, I'm cutting him loose, all right," says Amanda, pulling a pistol-gripped shotgun from beneath the seat. "You better believe I'm cutting him loose."

Amanda's father, a small-town attorney who supported his family by keeping the same drunks, car thieves, and various ne'er-do-wells out of jail from week to week, gave the shotgun to Amanda on her sixteenth birthday. Father and daughter spent an afternoon in a nearby pasture annihilating Mason jars and cardboard boxes placed on hay bales, Amanda growing more and more comfortable with the gun's heavy recoil and quickly learning to pump shells in and out of the firing chamber until she could discharge all five shells in a matter of seconds. Confident that Amanda was ready to remove the legs of anyone who might wish her harm, her father bought her a used Ford Pinto and placed the gun underneath one of his old army blankets in the hatch. Amanda has not fired the gun since the day of

training in the pasture, but it has followed her from car to car, always loaded, ready to redeem a bad situation.

"Now, sweetie, don't go getting crazy. You don't want to be messing up your life over some man," Sky advises. Amanda knows that the stranger is right, but the weight of the gun is comforting, summoning pleasant memories of her father, who taught her not to participate in any situation in which she did not have full control. She is not sure of her plan, but as she strides past the stranger, Amanda is certain of one thing: she is in control.

On a September day in 1971, Larry Yount trotted onto the artificial turf beneath the Houston Astrodome to warm up for what was to be the first game of his major league career. As he tossed his first warm-up pitch, he felt the muscles in his pitching arm shred like a brittle rope, and just like that, Larry's major league career was over before it began.

As Cameron reflects on what appears to be the end of his relationship with Amanda, he worries that a wonderful and fulfilling part of his future is being erased. He is bothered that he—like Larry Yount—will never know what might have been.* Cameron tells himself that he'll just have to be prepared for whatever his future holds.

Cameron is totally unprepared for the situation in which he now finds himself. Not only is Amanda standing in front of him pointing a shotgun at his face, but a small contingency of the Carolina Waves baseball team, flanked by two bikini-clad beauties, stands behind her, asking her not to do anything rash.

"Aren't you Billy Overby?" Cameron asks the man who appears to be Billy Overby.

Billy nods.

---

*Some readers will recall that Larry's brother, Robin Yount, enjoyed a long and successful career, becoming one of the few players in major league baseball to amass more than three thousand career hits.

"Great game last night," Cameron says, raising his hands above his head out of the assumption that gunpoint etiquette is the same regardless of one's relationship to the person holding the weapon.

"Thanks," Billy says softly, in deference to the woman with the shotgun.

"I'm Cameron and this is Amanda. We haven't been getting along the best lately."

"Now I wouldn't never have guessed that," chimes Mark Crocker, chasing his double negatives with a shot of bourbon. "You known her to shoot before?"

"Tell him I'll do it, Cameron," Amanda demands, sighting down the gun barrel at Cameron's chest.

"I'd have to say there's at least an outside chance she'll pull the trigger," Cameron says, his voice betraying the slightest bit of nervousness.

"That's not good enough, Cameron. Tell him you're one hundred percent certain that I will shoot if I want to," Amanda says.

"Amanda, honey, you don't need to do this. We'll work things out. We always do. You're scaring these people."

"Am I scaring you?"

"Of course you're scaring me. What if that gun went off accidentally right now? That would be tragic, wouldn't it?"

"Definitely tragic for you. Would you feel better if the gun were empty?" Amanda asks.

"We'd all feel much better if the gun were empty," Cameron says as Sky, Amber, and the trio of Waves nod in agreement.

"Ask me, then. Ask me to unload the gun."

"Amanda, honey, please unload the gun."

"Right now?"

"That would be nice."

"Anything for you, dear." Amanda lowers the gun's barrel until it is pointing at the heart of the port side of *Sam I Am*, and just as if the boat were nothing more than a large Mason jar on a bale of hay, she squeezes the trigger, blasting a hole just above the water line. She feels a surge of victorious adrenaline flood her body. With the second blast, the opiates of revenge begin to take effect; and by the time Amanda has discharged the fifth and final shell, she enjoys a nearly complete calm as she watches water rush into the football-sized hole in the side of the boat. Amanda tosses the gun to Cameron. "There, it's empty."

Full Count

Low and Away

A s Amanda drives west on Interstate 40, she debates how to react to having inflicted *Sam I Am* with a possibly mortal wound. She feels as if such a momentous act should be recognized in some way, if not by applause from the heavens, then at least by a blue light in her rear-view mirror, followed by several hours in pre-trial negotiations between her attorney and the DA.

After driving over twenty miles from the scene of the crime without any indication that the law is after her, or the slightest hint that she has angered even the most minor of gods, Amanda finds herself laughing. It is a laugh of liberation that comes from the depths of her belly and sends tears streaming down her face. When the laughter finally subsides, she thinks of her high school English teacher, Mr. Harrell, who for days on end preached about the insidious trap of revenge as the class struggled through the pages of *Moby Dick*. Amanda is now certain that Mr. Harrell knew nothing about the nature of revenge. As she waves giddily at a partially-toothed trucker whose wink would normally offend her, Amanda is certain that Captain Ahab died a happy death.

Back at the Sunrise Marina, Cameron stands beside a small pile of his worldly possessions: a file box of nautical maps; a paperback copy of *Swann's Way*; a knapsack containing his wallet, checkbook, birth certificate, and passport; a camera bag with camera, telephoto lens, and three rolls of film; a water-logged duffel bag of clothes; and a shaving kit which contains three disposable razors, sixty yards of mint-flavored dental floss, a small bottle of cologne, and a Willie Nelson cassette tape that Amber shoved in before tossing the shaving kit to Gary Ashton who stood on the dock and exercised his second baseman's fielding skills as the others salvaged what they could.

"Wouldn't have guessed she would have gone down so fast," says Mark Crocker, patting Cameron on the back as the group stares at the mast of *Sam I Am*, the only remaining part of the boat above the water line.

On a summer afternoon in 1919, Cleveland pitcher Ray Caldwell was one out from a road win against Philadelphia when a thunderstorm moved in. Because the end of the game was potentially near, the umpire allowed play to continue. Minutes later, as Caldwell wound up for a three and two pitch to Philadelphia shortstop John Dugan, a bolt of lightning struck Caldwell, knocking him from the mound into the infield, where he lay unconscious.

When he awoke five minutes later, Caldwell pleaded with Cleveland manager Charlie Mack to let him finish the game. Mack eventually conceded, and on the next pitch, Caldwell hurled a blistering fastball past Dugan for the win.

Caldwell appeared to retain his electrical charge for at least a year, winning twenty games for the Indians the following season.

Late last night, a storm very similar to the one that housed the bolt that struck Ray Caldwell, again moved through Philadelphia and is now headed for the southeastern coast. A slight breeze signifies the arrival of the front edge of the low-pressure system to the Sunrise Marina and causes the telltale atop the mast of *Sam I Am* to twitter.

The breeze plucks molecules from Cameron's dermis and carries them toward Billy Overby. Swarms of these molecules make their way through Overby's nasal passage and settle upon the mucus-coated cilia protruding from olfactory nerve cells in his epithelium. Once these molecules are absorbed in the mucus and attach to receptors, the cells fire off signals to Overby's olfactory bulbs, two knobby antennae extending from the front of the batting leader's

brain. From the olfactory bulbs, Cameron's scent—which has been misinterpreted as the scent of the abertam cheese Overby and his mother once sandwiched between saltine crackers—is relayed to the limbic system which regulates, among other things, emotions such as the heartsickness Overby now feels as palpable memories of his childhood erupt from the core of his mind.

In the spring of his fourth grade year, Billy returned home from Little League practice to find his mother and Ron, his mother's first romantic interest since her husband's death, packing boxes.

"You're just in time to help," Ron said as he tossed a box of Billy's clothes across the living room, careful not to spill from the bottle of beer in his hand.

"Oh, honey, I have the best news; we're moving to Richmond," said his mother with an unconvincing smile. "Ron's got a great job lined up, and the weather's a lot nicer there."

"What about my friends?"

"They'll still be your friends, and you'll make lots of new friends in Richmond."

Billy felt his world slipping out from under him. "If it's Ron's job, why does he need us to go?"

"It's the best thing right now, Billy. I promise."

Billy wanted to believe his mother, but he wasn't sure she believed herself.

After two days of packing boxes, loading the rented moving van, and a trip to Dr. Van Horn's office, the trio was off, Billy's arm in a sling as a result of a strained muscle in his upper arm he incurred as he and Ron fought to negotiate the sofa through the front door.

Not only did things not improve in Richmond, they got worse. Much worse. The job Ron had boasted of turned out to be non-existent, and all that Ron had waiting for him in Richmond was a bunch of old drinking buddies and an ex-girlfriend. The money that Ron and Billy's mother had saved for the move quickly ran out, and his mother took a job cleaning office buildings in the early mornings. Ron found a job working for one of his old friends as a roofer. They could have made ends meet pretty well if Ron had not spent as much time at bars as he did atop houses. But Billy was always glad to hear Ron stomping out of the house to the bar because it meant that Billy would have his mother all to himself for the night.

Mornings, he'd awake to find a freshly penned I-love-you note from his mother, who left before sunrise to clean several of Richmond's office buildings. Then Billy would dress and face the part of the day he dreaded most, breakfast with a hungover Ron, who would lecture Billy on how easy he had it, how fourth grade was a cakewalk compared to doing real work all day and how Billy had sure as hell better appreciate the sweat that went into earning his lunch money and buying his new shoes.

"Yes, sir, thank you," Billy would respond as he prayed for Ron's sudden death.

And things got worse.

Billy opened the door one morning to a bleached-blonde stick figure dressed in a bikini top and a skirt that covered very little of her scrawny thighs.

"Well, hello there, handsome. Is your daddy home?"

"My father's dead," Billy said.

The woman laughed and flipped loose strands of bleached hair behind her ear. "I mean Ron. Is Ron home?"

Billy looked over his shoulder to see Ron stomping toward them.

"Damn it, Shelia. What are you doing here?"

"I thought you might want to have a little fun before work."

 *Full Count*

"Jesus Christ, Shelia. You could have waited for the boy to leave for the school bus."

Shelia turned to Billy. "You don't have anything against people having fun, do you, sweetie?"

Billy said nothing.

"Damn it, boy, the lady's talking to you."

Still Billy said nothing.

Ron slapped Billy stiffly in the back of the head. "What have I told you about behaving yourself? Now get going to the bus stop."

"It's not time yet," Billy said, holding his hands to his head to shield himself from another blow.

"Go to your room, then. And don't come out until I tell you."

Billy gladly obliged and went to his room where he lay on his bed with the lights off and listened to a cassette of mixed songs he and his mother had made for the trip to Richmond.

"And this song is for my darling Billy," came his mother's voice, followed by the opening chords of "You and Me Against the World."

To say his mother meant the world to Billy would not be an overstatement, and if the two had been close in Roanoke, that closeness had only grown with the move to Richmond, Billy having left behind his friends and, until his arm was out of the sling, baseball. Until his arrival in Richmond, Billy had always enjoyed school, but now he spent weekdays being tormented by the twenty-six children of Miss Jan Thornberry's fourth-grade class. His very first day at Pine View Elementary School, Billy had accidentally knocked over a wicker planter as the class marched single file on their return from morning recess. Billy scurried to right the planter, but with his right arm in the sling, he only managed to cause further damage to the dislodged impatiens.

Miss Thornberry made Billy wait for the janitor while she marched the rest of the students back to the classroom.

After a few minutes, a pale, fleshy man in a blue jumpsuit arrived with broom, dustpan, and trashcan. "You got something against flowers, kid?" the corpulent custodian asked as he surveyed the damage.

"No, sir, I didn't mean to knock them over."

"Well, that's good. If you'd made this mess on purpose, I'm afraid I would've had to kill you."

"I'm sorry, sir." Billy said, imagining himself sprinting the many miles back to Roanoke, back to his best friend, Stephen Brooks, and back to Ms. Parrish, in Billy's mind the nicest, most beautiful teacher one could ever hope for, her melodic voice standing in sharp contrast to the long list of nasal warnings Miss Thornberry had bombarded him with that morning.

"Hey, lighten up, kid. I'm just joking. A little dirt on the floor never hurt nobody. And don't 'sir' me. If I wanted to be called 'sir,' I'd have picked a different profession. My name's George," the janitor said, handing Billy the dustpan.

As George swept, creating tiny furrows of soil along the speckled tiles of the floor, Billy held the dustpan and studied George's tattoo. Two snakes, one a vibrant green and the other a deep red, enlivened the pale flesh of George's right forearm. The serpents formed an oval as the green snake swallowed the tail of the red snake and the red snake returned the favor, swallowing the tail of its counterpart with its crimson-scaled mouth.

The image intrigued Billy. It puzzled him. To what extent could the two serpents devour each other? He tried to break the problem apart by imagining the red snake swallowing all but the head of the green snake. He then imagined the green snake swallowing all but the head of

the red, thus swallowing most of himself, as well. And here things fell apart. Billy started over, this time with the green snake swallowing first, but before he could have the snakes ingest themselves, George was patting him on the back.

"You better be getting back to class. You don't want to be getting on Miss Thornberry's bad side."

"Does she have a good side?"

George laughed. "I'm sure it's in there somewhere."

When Billy returned to the classroom, Miss Thornberry's good side was nowhere to be found. Billy was told he was to write the sentence, "We will learn how to walk in an orderly fashion," two hundred times in his best handwriting. Billy's heart sank when he looked at the paper of the girl in front of him and realized that the rest of the class had been given the same assignment. By punishing the entire class, Miss Thornberry had destroyed whatever chance he had of making new friends.

But when Billy was alone with his mother, all of his problems shrank away. As the last notes of "You and Me against the World" faded, his mother's voice returned, her heavy breathing reminding Billy of how they had danced around the living room floor as they made the tape.

"Lya, lya, lya," chimed his mother's voice.

"Lya, lya, lya," Billy responded, mouthing the words as they played on the tape.

LYA. Love you always.

As James Taylor strummed the opening chords of "You've Got a Friend," Billy shut his eyes and let his head sink into his pillow, but the peaceful sway was soon interrupted by less than peaceful sounds from the other room. Billy had no idea what the guttural grunts and groans emitting from Ron and the woman signified, but even the intermingled laughter contained a maniacal undertone that Billy intuited as being against his mother, and therefore, against himself.

Billy hummed along with James Taylor in an effort to ignore the sounds, but the harder he tried to ignore the intruding noise, the more invasive it became.

Billy decided to investigate. He rose from his bed, opened his bedroom door, and made his way toward the strange sounds.

What Billy found were two nude adults who appeared to be attempting to swallow each other like the snakes on Janitor George's forearm. The ferocity with which they went at each other struck Billy as odd, primarily because he had never seen Ron do anything with much enthusiasm.

The woman turned her head and pushed her hair out of her face. Then she saw Billy. She sprang from Ron and grabbed her shirt from the sofa.

Ron's face tightened. "Goddamnit, what did I tell you, boy!" he yelled, making no attempt to clothe himself as he rose and started toward Billy. Billy darted to his bedroom, slammed his door shut, and locked it as Ron cursed from the other side.

"You mention one damn word of this to your mother and you'll both be sorry," warned Ron. "You hear me?"

Billy said nothing.

"I'm as serious as I can be," Ron iterated. "I'll kill you."

Billy remained in his room. After the opening and closing of the front door signaled the exit of the woman, and shortly thereafter, Ron, Billy fell into a light and restless sleep which was eventually broken by the sounds of his mother returning from work at mid-morning. Billy listened as his mother made her way to the kitchen. He heard the fizz of soda and the clink of a knife against the mayonnaise jar. He wanted to run to her, but he had no idea what he would say. He listened to her feet fall near his door as she walked toward the sofa, and then he heard something more disturbing than he had heard all morning.

He heard his mother cry.

His mother's sobs were not without music. They formed a soft but painful melody, and the gasps that broke the sobs formed a rhythm filled with unbridled despair. The sobs pulled Billy from his room, and when his mother saw him, she instinctively hid the anguish from her face. "What are you doing home, sweetheart?" she asked, forcing her tear-streaked cheeks into a smile.

"I wasn't feeling good."

"Ron should have called me."

Billy took a seat on the sofa beside his mother. "Why were you crying, Mom?"

"Oh, honey, I don't know. I was just being a big old baby, I guess. I had such high hopes, and things haven't been going all that great."

"I know," Billy said, thinking of the note he had found in his desk the week before at school. As Miss Thornberry covered the board with math problems, Billy had grown warm with excitement as he read the note: "Billy, I think you are really neat. I also think you are cute. Do you like me?" It was signed by Shelley Langdon, an angelic girl, who besides being the prettiest girl in his class, was also one of the few classmates who ever treated Billy with the least bit of kindness, once even offering him a seat beside her in the cafeteria.

Billy read the purple-inked letter twice more, and then penned a response as the rest of the class worked away at long division.

It took most of the recess period for Billy to gather the courage to make his way across the playground to deliver his note to Shelley, but as he approached the tether ball pole around which Shelley and her friends were gathered, his confidence grew with the anticipation of the great social leap he was about to make. Not only was romance about to enter his life, but he was certain the teasing from other students would end once he was the boyfriend of the prettiest girl in the entire fourth grade.

Billy reached the group of girls and handed the note to Shelley. As she unfolded it, Billy walked as casually as he could to a nearby maple and took a seat in its shade.

Shelley read the note intently, but she did not react as Billy had expected. Rather than appearing happy that her love was requited, she appeared merely confused. Very confused.

Then Billy noticed Andy Reddick, Martin Lance, and Frankie Parker observing the situation from the edge of the basketball court. They bent over in laughter as a seemingly bewildered Shelley handed Billy's note to Angela Newberry for a second opinion.

By the time the bell rang to end recess, Billy realized he'd been had. The author of the note he had found in his desk was not Shelley Langdon, but Andy Reddick and crew.

As the other children filed back into the school building, Billy sprinted across the playground in the opposite direction. He ran until he reached the bus parking lot where he climbed under bus number seventeen. Once he was discovered by a teacher's aide on a smoking break, it took almost a half hour of coaxing from Principal Whitherspoon to unglue the humiliation that kept his back pushed against the dusty rubber of one of the bus's rear tires.

"Yeah, I know what you mean. I miss Roanoke," Billy said to his mother.

"Maybe this move was a bad idea after all. We'll all sit down and talk about things when Ron gets home tonight," she said, cupping his face in her hands.

"Mom?"

"Yes, dear?"

"Ron was with a woman."

"What do you mean, honey?"

As Billy explained the events of the morning, Billy was pleased that rather than hurting his mother, the information seemed to excite her.

"That pathetic little bastard," she said, taking Billy by the hand. "Come on, we've got some packing to do."

By four that afternoon, Billy and his mother had packed all of their belongings and gone on a shopping spree with Ron's credit cards. They spent the miles back to Roanoke singing with the radio as Billy used his newly purchased pocketknife to carve chunks from a wedge of abertam cheese, placing the chunks on saltine crackers and feeding them alternately to his mother and himself.

That evening, Billy drifted toward sleep in the Roanoke Holiday Inn, his head on his mother's lap, the two of them lit by the black and white glow of an old *Honeymooners* episode, and the faint scent of abertam cheese drifting in the hope-filled air.

After making arrangements with a salvage company to pull *Sam I Am* from her submerged mooring, Cameron returns Mark Crocker's cell phone and thanks everyone for their help.

"And thanks for an exciting start to our day," says Mark Crocker.

Amber and Sky give Cameron a pat on the back and wish him good luck.

"Yeah, best of luck," Billy Overby says as another bundle of Cameron's molecules assaults his olfactory system, the faux abertam cheese aroma sending Billy back to the feelings of relief and joy that had been so abundant upon his return to Roanoke, where his arm healed and his mother never again made such an erroneous choice in men.

As Billy makes his way to *Screwball III*, the nostalgia begins to fade, and finding himself unready to end his excursion to the past, he turns back to Cameron and his bouquet. "Hey, want to go fishing?"

"Yeah, I'd love to," Cameron says.

"What do you say, Mark, mind if he comes along?"

"All right by me, as long as he don't cause nobody to shoot my boat."

As Cameron sits atop his duffel on the deck of *Screwball III*, drinking bourbon with Sky, Amber, Billy Overby, and Gary Ashton, he finds himself laughing.

"You must have a pretty good sense of humor," Amber says, pulling a t-shirt over her bikini top as a cloud moves across the morning sun. "What are you thinking about?"

Cameron tosses a chunk of chicken to a seagull keeping speed alongside *Screwball III*, as Mark Crocker throttles the boat past a channel marker into the open sea. "I was just thinking that last night I was on my boat imagining a baseball game, and now my boat's not much more than a memory and the Carolina Waves, three of them at least, are real. That's kind of crazy, don't you think?"

Sky nods. "It's a strange world. That's sure enough."

"What's the strangest thing about it, Sky?" asks Billy, his Cameron-triggered boyhood memories giving way to the image of Sky stabbing her ex-husband.

"Oh, honey, take your pick. How about you being a millionaire because you can swing a bat? That's pretty strange."

"Yeah, I agree," says Billy. "But surely there are plenty of things stranger than that."

"How about sex?" Amber chimes in.

"What's strange about sex?" challenges Gary Ashton.

Amber snaps back, "Maybe you and me need to go

back to that cabin so I can show you just how strange it can be."

"No arguments here," says Gary, springing to his feet and offering a hand to Amber.

"This won't take long," Amber says, allowing Gary to help her up and lead her through the door of the main cabin.

"So this is life in the big leagues?" Cameron says, taking the chair Amber vacated.

"This is life in the big leagues when you're around Mark Crocker, at least," Billy says.

"Now don't go putting everything off on Mark," says Sky. "Besides, he sure isn't the first one to come up with the formula of baseball, booze, and women. Cameron's no ballplayer, but he likes the women, too, I bet. At least when they aren't shooting off shotguns in his direction."

Cameron laughs, but finds his mood darkening. "Those clouds look a bit threatening," he says, pointing off the starboard bow.

"Don't go changing the subject. Tell us about your shooter friend."

"I don't want to talk about it right now," Cameron says.

"Tell us something else, then. Entertain us. Tell us about the other women of your life."

"Maybe in a little while," Cameron says, traveling back through the years until he collides with Mrs. Rodriguez, his boyhood neighbor and first love.

As the first drops of rain begin to fall, Cameron's memories of Raquel Rodriguez grow more vivid, and his mood lightens.

Full Count

Rain Delay

As Raquel Rodriguez looked out her kitchen window to check the water level in the birdbath, she knew that she was not really checking the water level in the bird bath, but rather stealing another glimpse of fifteen-year-old Cameron Lawrence, whose glistening body paced row by row through her backyard, his old lawnmower kicking up a cloud of dust and filling the air with the cough of its engine. It was the third time Cameron had cut the grass since she and her husband moved into the neighborhood a month earlier. Cameron had refused payment for the first two mowings, but today she would insist that he take fifteen dollars for his hard work.

Satisfied with the amount of water in the birdbath which she was not really checking, Raquel decided to make lemonade. She began by slicing the dozen lemons she had picked up at the grocery store, nice plump symmetrical lemons unlike the authentically disfigured ones that used to grow on the trees of her childhood in Tucson, but the citrus mist that sprang from the peel as the blade passed through was more than enough to turn the air of her kitchen into the air of her mother's kitchen, and Raquel held the hopefulness of a young girl in her heart as she juiced the lemons and brought the sugar water to a boil. She was enjoying her mother's cheerful singing when Cameron's voice brought her back to the present.

"All finished, Mrs. Rodriguez," he called from the porch.

"Come in, Cameron," bid Raquel.

A bare-chested Cameron opened the screen door and stepped into the kitchen. Raquel detected no self-consciousness on the boy's part as he surveyed her kitchen, his gaze seeming to give extra attention to the rosemary plant on the windowsill.

"I'm making lemonade. Won't you stay and have a glass?" Raquel asked as the boy's musk filled her kitchen and once again threw her back in time, past the last four years of her deteriorating marriage, past her two miscarriages, past her mother's death, back to her teenage romance with Raul Mercado. As Raquel moved the sugar water from the burner, she thought how much Cameron resembled a paler version of Raul. "I'll be right back," she said, and as she went to the bedroom to get the fifteen dollars she was going to insist Cameron take for cutting the lawn, she thought about the summer night in the pine forest of Mt. Lemmon, high above Tucson, of the fire Raul had built and how he had taken her, taken her as a man takes a woman he loves, there on a blanket by the fire, and how he had been so strong and at the same time so gentle, and how all of her friends had said she would not enjoy her first time and how absolutely wrong they had been, how she had cried as Raul shivered above her and then let his head drop onto her breast, and how Raul had kissed her wet cheeks and sworn his eternal love.

And here she fought to keep time frozen, to keep it from creeping back toward the present, for it was only weeks later that Raul was stabbed as he stepped between two drunks fighting over something she could not remember, or perhaps she never knew, never wanted to know what paltry prize had resulted in the death of her truest love.

Looking at the framed photo of herself and her husband, she remembered the one time she had told Enrique Rodriguez about her murdered love because she felt it important to disclose that part of herself to the man who had proposed marriage, and how Enrique had slapped her across the face with the back of his hand and told her that he never again wanted to hear her speak of having been with another man.

When Raquel returned with the fifteen dollars, she

stopped short of the kitchen, because as far as she could trust her nose, it was her beloved, deceased Raul whose scent was floating from the kitchen into the hall. She took a deep breath and stepped into the masculine aroma.

"Everything all right?" Cameron asked.

"Yes, yes. Everything is wonderful," Raquel assured the boy as her heart grew inside her. "Here, I want you to have this."

"No, I told you last time, I'm not taking it."

"I will be sad if you do not let me pay you."

"Why?" Cameron asked.

"Because if you will not allow me to pay you, then I will not allow you to continue to cut my grass, and I will have to do it myself."

"Well, maybe instead of paying me, you can just do something for me sometime," Cameron said as Raquel stirred the juice of the lemons into the sugar water.

"And what could I possibly do for someone as young and strong as you?" Raquel said, dropping ice cubes into two glasses.

"You could give me a kiss."

Raquel was stunned. She had not meant to lead the boy on. Not consciously, at least. "That is an awfully bold suggestion," she said, pouring lemonade into the two glasses.

"I'm sorry, Mrs. Rodriguez. I had no idea I was going to say that."

"Do not apologize, Cameron. My mother used to say that slips of the tongue are shouts from the heart." Raquel handed Cameron a glass of lemonade. "But I'm afraid you will have to take the fifteen dollars, for I cannot grant your request."

"Because you are married?"

"Because you are only a boy, and boys are meant to kiss young girls."

"But what if I want to kiss you, instead?"

"Then you will have to wait until you are a man."

"Then I'll wait, and you can owe me," Cameron said, gulping the lemonade and hurrying out of the kitchen before Raquel could give him the fifteen dollars.

For the next two years Cameron continued to cut the Rodriguez's grass, but there were no more awkward moments over lemonade. A bond of genuine friendship formed between Raquel and the boy that became an important lifeline for Raquel as her marriage to Enrique continued to deteriorate, and an important anchor for Cameron as his parents' evening cocktails began to take the form of full-blown alcoholism.

Gradually, Enrique's evenings at the office grew longer and his business trips became more frequent. On the evenings Enrique was away, Cameron would stay and watch movies until the early morning, asking endless questions about Raquel's childhood in Tucson and creating outlandish ice cream sundaes, her favorite of which was Cameron's s'more sundae, vanilla ice cream covered in crumbled graham crackers, marshmallows, and a warm chocolate sauce.

One evening as Raquel and Cameron watched a network presentation of *The Way We Were* and finished off a second round of butterscotch and Hershey bar sundaes, Cameron handed her a scrap of paper, wrinkled and a bit dirty, with several dozen faded pencil hatch marks.

"What's this?" Raquel asked.

"I'm collecting on an I.O.U."

"For what?"

"It's all of the kisses you owe me. I'm turning eighteen next week, and I figure as an official adult I can start collecting."

Raquel remembered the fifteen-year-old Cameron of only a few years earlier and smiled. "You do, do you?"

"I assume you're good for it."

Raquel set the remnants of her butterscotch-Hershey sundae on the end table beside the sofa. "Come here," she said. She had intended to place an innocent kiss on Cameron's forehead, but as she leaned toward him, Cameron seized her lips with his. As he lowered himself on top of her, she did not resist. Perhaps it was because it had been a long time since she felt so urgently wanted by a man, or maybe it was because for over two years she had been haunted by the scent of Raul Mercado that filled the room when Cameron was around, or maybe it was simply that it felt so good, but for whatever reasons, she gave in completely.

Cameron attacked her body like a young boy peeling the paper from his Christmas presents. He smiled broadly as he slid her panties down her legs and slipped them over her bare feet, then quickly worked his way back up her legs with quick staccato kisses, slowing as he moved along her thighs until his enthusiastic tongue began a thorough exploration of her cortina mágica. As a girl, Raquel's mother had taught her that her cortina mágica was the door to all of her womanly enchantment, and as Cameron licked softly at the folds of the magic curtain, she found it easy to believe her mother had been right.

Cameron had found his explorations no less exciting than she. He walked his hands up the sofa, and Raquel watched him guide his erection into her as she noted that his was the palest member to ever be inside her. Cameron kissed her eyes as he filled her mind and body.

"I love you," he whispered into her ear.

Raquel smiled. "And I love you, you silly, wonderful boy."

Their sexual escapades would be fervent and frequent for the next two months. While Enrique Rodriguez was never present enough to become suspicious of Raquel's newfound cheer, the romance was finally discovered by Cameron's mother, Yvonne Lawrence, when she happened upon the lovers in the Rodriguez's backyard on one of her drunken, midnight stumblings.

Raquel was straddling Cameron when she heard the ice cubes of Yvonne's gin and tonic clinking around the boxwoods that separated their yards. Raquel and Cameron froze as Yvonne seemed to stare just long enough to insure she could trust her sight. Then she returned to the Lawrence's yard with a shriek of laughter. Before Raquel could move, Cameron pulled her back down onto his *varita mágica*. Within seconds, Raquel was panting at the quarter moon and shivering with delight.

Two weeks later Cameron left for college, and when his letter arrived mid-term saying he might be falling in love with a fair-headed Swedish boy named Alex, she was happy for Cameron and wrote him a poem about the night under the moon that she would keep forever near her heart.

A year later Raquel left Enrique and moved to a small town in South Carolina where she met Paul Walker. Within two months, the two were married and had opened what would become a very successful market for the growing Hispanic community.

Resume Play

For Cameron, the thrill of a day on storm-churned seas dissipates with each mile he moves west behind the wheel of Mark Crocker's Suburban.

"Not much company, are they?" says Sky, looking back from the passenger seat to inventory their well-liquored companions.

"It was a rough day out there today."

Sky laughs. "I don't think their day was quite as rough as yours. You're the one who lost his home today, and you're the one who got us through the storm. If things had been left up to our drunken Captain Crocker, we might all be bobbing in the middle of the ocean right now."

"He wasn't doing such a bad job before he passed out." Cameron laughs nervously. He has noticed that as they move towards Raleigh, the towns grow closer together. Already he feels the knots of claustrophobia gathering in his chest. He draws a slow, deep breath in an effort to chase the knots away, but they only cinch tighter with his exhalation. When Sky lights a cigarette, he asks if she might have one for him.

"You smoke?"

"Not for a while. But this seems like a pretty good time to start."

The ringing phone jackhammers through Billy Overby's hangover until the answering machine stops the onslaught after the fourth ring. As Billy listens to his own voice greet the caller, he can feel his pulse beating a steady rhythm against the inside of his skull and notices that his tongue seems to be glued to the bottom of his parched mouth.

When his mother's voice speaks to him through the answering machine, Billy reaches for the phone. "Hi, Mom."

"Hello, dear. You sound like you just woke up."

Billy glances at the clock. A quarter after eleven. Four hours later than he usually wakes. "No, I've been up for a while. I just went out for a jog."

"On a game day? You don't usually jog on game days."

"I thought I'd try something new."

"Are you feeling okay? You don't sound so good, honey."

"I'm fine, Mom."

"I was going to go down and check on things at the soup kitchen, but I could stop by and fix you some lunch if you like."

"I'm fine, Mom."

"Okay, if you say so, but try to rest this afternoon before the game. By the way, I got a letter from Mary Ellington in today's mail. She says people ask her all the time what kind of math student you were. She says she tells them she's sure you have no problem figuring out your batting statistics."

"I wish she'd been that nice to me in high school."

"She was just doing her job. Are you sure you're feeling all right?"

"I told you, Mom, I'm fine. You go on down to the soup kitchen."

"Okay, but you call me if you get to feeling bad, and I want you to just go out there and enjoy yourself tonight, you hear?"

"I will, Mom."

"I love you, Billy."

"I love you, Mom."

Billy hangs up the phone and heads for the kitchen to

address his hangover. Exiting his bedroom, he is startled by a figure on the couch eating a bowl of cereal and watching television.

Cameron can tell by the look on Billy's face that at some point during his drunken sleep Billy forgot about his invitation to Cameron to stay the night. "I'm sorry. I meant to leave a while ago. It'll just take a second to get my things together."

Images of the previous day's boating adventures begin to make their way through Billy's aching head. As the ocean had grown rougher, Crocker had grown more and more determined not to end the fishing trip prematurely. As the other boats had passed by on their way to safe harbor, Crocker had issued toots on the air horn, the wind swallowing his drunken shouts of inquiry concerning the whereabouts of the bluefish and mackerels.

"I guess you're used to rough seas, huh?" Billy had asked Cameron.

"You never get used to seas like this."

"Should we be heading back in?"

Cameron had paused and looked up, studying Crocker in the cockpit smiling wildly into the wind and rain. "I don't think it really matters what we should do. I don't think he's going to turn around."

For the first time in a long time, Billy had been frightened. Looking out into the choppy foam, he realized the ocean had no idea that he was the top batter in professional baseball. The ocean didn't care that throngs of young boys lined up in malls for his autograph or that his rookie baseball card, nothing more than a small square of cardboard covered in colored ink, was worth more than twelve hundred dollars.

Billy, although not a heavy drinker and baffled by how some of his teammates could put away large daily quantities of alcohol and still perform on the field, had decided to drink more heavily in an effort to chase away the fear that was brewing in his chest. But rather than helping matters, the bourbon and the tossing of the boat resulted in full-blown seasickness. With his head sticking through the boat's railing, Billy's fear only swelled as he looked down into the angry ocean between retches.

And things got worse. From his prone position, Billy had watched the bow of *Screwball III* plough straight up the oncoming waves and then hurtle down the backside of the growing swells, but he began to notice that the boat was no longer taking the waves head on. The boat was being pitched sideways and hurled off course each time a wave met it broadside, and Billy Overby grew more and more convinced that his hitting streak was going to end on the floor of the Atlantic Ocean.

His death became more of a certainty when a nearby thud interrupted one of his retching spells and he turned to see that Mark Crocker had somehow been launched from the steering cockpit onto the deck beside Billy. Crocker reeked of bourbon and insanity, and it took a concerted effort by the others to convince Crocker to lie still while they assessed his injuries.

While Gary, Sky, and Amber blotted scattered patches of blood, Cameron went up to the cockpit. "We've lost power," he announced from up above.

Billy began to pray. He prayed to a god who had taken his father from him at an early age. He prayed to a god who had blessed him with the unending love of a wonderful mother, to a god who had given him the talent to be the leading hitter in professional baseball, who had given him Mark Crocker as a friend, and who had, on this day, created the ocean that threatened to swallow him within the half hour. Before Billy could get his prayer fully formed, a voice called from above.

"Anybody have a bobby pin?" Cameron had removed a panel from the steering console to reveal a tangled array of multi-colored wires.

Sky and Amber looked at each other, shaking their heads.

"Never mind. Somebody bring me that tackle box," Cameron instructed, pointing at the metal tackle box at Billy's feet.

Billy grabbed the large, red box and lunged for the cockpit ladder. As he navigated the nine rungs up to the cockpit, it took all of his world-class concentration to hold his retching down and to keep his feet on the ladder. He was two rungs from the top when the starboard side dipped abruptly toward the water; but just when Billy was certain he was headed overboard, Cameron grabbed a fistful of Billy's shirt and yanked him up to the cockpit platform.

Without a word, Cameron removed a large hook and a pair of pliers from the tackle box. In a matter of seconds he had straightened the hook and stuck it through a purple rubber worm, making a makeshift length of insulated wire which he connected to two posts underneath the console.

"That should do it," he said, turning the ignition key.

Billy heard a low rumble beneath the blowing wind; and as the faint smell of abertam cheese sifted through his nostrils, he allowed himself to think that they just might make it out of the storm.

Cameron takes his shaving kit from the coffee table and stuffs it into his bulging duffle bag. "Thanks again for letting me stay here last night."

Billy recalls the gratitude he had felt as Cameron piloted *Screwball III* back into safe harbor. "Thanks for getting us back to the marina. We probably would have died if you hadn't been with us."

"Maybe, but I promise I was just as happy as you were that we didn't go down. Could I use your phone? I need to call a cab."

"Where you going to go?"

"I haven't figured that out yet."

"You can stay here for another night or two if you want."

"I appreciate the offer, but I should get out of your hair. You've got a lot on your mind these days, I'm sure." The scene felt surreal to Cameron. Three days ago he would have bet his testicles that he wouldn't be standing in Billy Overby's house making small talk. Then again, three days ago he hadn't even thought about the possibility of losing *Sam I Am*.

"No, really, you should stay here for a few days. If it would make you feel better you could help out around the house. I had to fire my lawn guy last week, so there's plenty that needs to be done. Take a look."

Billy and Cameron step out onto the patio.

"Why'd you have to fire the lawn guy?"

"He had a drinking problem."

"I thought lawn guys were supposed to have drinking problems."

"It was pretty bad. He passed out on the riding mower and ran through the fence," Billy says, pointing to a missing section of the high wooden fence that surrounds the back yard. "Mrs. Johnson next door was out tending her roses and barely escaped."

"How about her roses?"

"They weren't so lucky."

By the time Billy is ready to leave for the ballpark, Cameron has managed to piece together most of the damaged section of fence.

  *Full Count*

"You sure you don't want to go to the game?" Billy calls from the patio.

"Yeah, thanks. Have a great game."

"Okay, I'll make sure there's a ticket at the will call window if you change your mind."

Billy Overby sits in front of his locker drinking a cup of coffee, praying between sips. Having been to fewer than a dozen church services in his life, Billy prays for the simple reason that it feels as if someone is listening. He once heard a televangelist say that to effectively talk to God, one has to address him by name. The televangelist had said God's name is Yahweh, but the preacher then suggested that a fifty-dollar donation would put one on better terms with Yahweh. Billy decides his God is called Bob.

Bob, thanks for not letting me drown yesterday. Bless my mother. Bless my swing. Bob rules. Amen.

Having finished his temporary repair of the fence, Cameron decides to mow Billy's lawn. The riding mower appears to be out of commission from the fence run-in, but Cameron finds a push mower in the back of the garage.

The large oaks in the backyard remind Cameron of his college campus and how much it had hurt to leave Raquel Rodriguez. He had spent his first afternoon walking the brick walks of the campus. Around him young people threw Frisbees, lay on towels as they spread tanning lotion on one another, tossed lacrosse, and generally seemed to enjoy being in college. He tried to force the same enthusiasm into himself, but all he could think about was Raquel Rodriguez. He could feel her in his mouth and on his chest. He could feel their pelvises pressed together in ecstasy. He could hear her laugh.

After a twenty minute wait in line outside the campus bookstore seemed to move him no closer to the doors, he gave up on being a college student for the day and returned to his dormitory.

As he walked down the tiled hallway, the collective noise of dozens of males echoed against the cinderblock walls. He glanced quickly into each room as he passed and was struck with the notion that he felt himself to be much older than these other men, these boys, shouting at video games, playing cards, and guzzling cheap beer.

On his door were two baseball mitts made out of construction paper, one inscribed with his name, the other inscribed, he supposed, with the name of his roommate who had not yet arrived, Alex Lindgren.

Cameron loved baseball but the construction paper mitts oozed of grade school, intensifying his feeling that by going to college he had stepped backwards chronologically.

The room was bare. Other than putting sheets on his stained single mattress, he had done nothing to move in. A suitcase and a cardboard crate sat beside his bed.

Cameron kicked the suitcase so that it fell flat on the floor. He unzipped it, pulled out a hardcover edition of *Leaves of Grass*, and removed his only picture of Raquel from between its pages.

In the photo, Raquel was sitting on one of her kitchen chairs, leaning forward in a loving smile as she pled with Cameron not to snap the picture. Her olive legs rose to her short nightgown and her hair was tousled in morning disarray.

Also in the pages was an envelope containing several locks of Raquel's hair, which she had snipped only minutes before he left her.

Cameron sat on his bed, pulling the silky threads through his fingers. He wished he were with her at her house, not in

a concrete box with a hundred pimply males. He lay back on his bed and shut his eyes, willing his imagination to create Raquel for him. He imagined his nose nuzzling into her neck. He ran a finger over her delicate collar bone. He tried to feel her lips brush his shoulder.

His imagination was more than up to the task, and it wasn't long before Cameron held his hardness in his hand. He could hear her now. Her moans sent shivers through his legs, and within moments he and Raquel climaxed triumphantly.

Cameron had just begun to wake from his post-coital nap when there was a knock at the door.

"Hello. Alex Lindgren. You must be Cameron Lawrence," said the small blonde male in the doorway. He was wearing a back pack nearly as large as he was.

"That's me," said Cameron. "You need a hand with anything?"

"Got it all right here," said Alex, making his way into the room and depositing his pack on the other single mattress.

That night, while Alex sat on his bed reading *The Catcher in the Rye*, Cameron sat at one of the ancient wooden desks writing to Raquel. The desk was decorated with scratched initials and rock lyrics courtesy of prior occupants.

Greetings Princess,

What are you doing and why am I not with you? I hope you're having a drink for us.

I met my roommate today, Alex Lindgren, by all early indications a pretty decent guy. A little quiet, but bright. I'm thankful that he's not some Neanderthal. Or maybe I wish he were. Maybe that would be the final straw and I'd pack up and come back to you where I belong.

Classes begin tomorrow, and I am hoping that it will help to shove dates, formulas, and dead authors into my head so that I will have at least a bit of relief from this constant longing for you.

I worry that you already know what I am afraid to know, that what we "have" will soon be what we "had." I cannot imagine it being true, but that's how lives work, isn't it? It seems so ridiculous to be apart in the name of education and enlightenment. When I am with you I know all I will ever need to know.

Tonight I'll watch the Braves game, and then Alex and I are going to a party off campus that he was invited to. I'm not expecting my first college social outing to consist of much more than small, smoky rooms and lots of drunk people, but maybe I will be surprised. I doubt it.

If you could write and tell me that my concerns about our future are silly, I would be so relieved, but I know you will do this only if you can do it with certainty. I know you will not give me false hope.

I love you, Raquel,

C

Cameron put the note in an envelope and sealed it, then retrieved the photograph of Raquel from the top drawer of his desk.

"And who is that?" Alex asked, peering over his book.

"Oh, this is Raquel."

"Raquel. I see." Alex put down his book and walked over to Cameron's desk. "She's attractive. Is she your girlfriend?"

"I guess you could say that. For now, at least."

"You love her. I can tell."

"How?"

"I just can. It hurts you to look at her picture."

Cameron did not know how to respond. Alex went to

his pack and fished a small photo from one of the zippered side pockets. He handed it to Cameron.

"This is Justin. I loved him. And now he's gone."

"What happened?"

"He was murdered outside a bar."

Cameron looked at the photo. The young man was light in his hair and complexion. He looked a good deal like Alex. "Your brother?"

Alex let out a small snort. "No, not my brother. My boyfriend."

"Oh, I see."

"Ah, you are surprised. I can tell."

"Well, yeah, I guess I am."

More than anything, Cameron was curious. He had never known a gay person, not personally, at least as far as he knew.

"Does it bother you?" Alex asked, a bit of defensiveness leaking into his voice.

"No, I don't think so," Cameron said.

Dr. Lewis Eldenham stood in the lecture room pointing to a slide of men playing rugby on a muddy field. "What is it that the human psyche finds appealing about sports?"

None of the students in the Introduction to Sociology class volunteered a response.

Cameron pondered the question. He himself had just used one of the computers in the undergraduate library to place two ten dollar bets on the Atlanta Braves' doubleheader against the Red Sox. He raised his hand.

"Ah, yes," boomed Dr. Eldenham.

Cameron cleared his throat. "Sports provide the illusion of order and fairness."

"Interesting," said Dr. Eldenham, giving his beard a quick stroke. "Can you elaborate?"

Cameron felt the eyes room turn toward him. "In

the real world, fairness plays a limited role. The best job candidate may lose out to the son of the employer's childhood friend. On Wall Street, people can make millions of dollars by breaking the rules. But in sports, the lines are straight and players who break the rules are penalized." He was about to say more when he was interrupted by someone in the back of the room.

"I thought we played sports to get chicks!" exclaimed the anonymous voice. The class laughed. Cameron joined in.

"I think you're both on the right track," Dr. Eldenham said with a grin. "I want the rest of you to think about it, as well." He assigned a five hundred word essay on the topic and dismissed class.

Cameron entered his room to find that he was not alone.

"Oh, Cameron, hi. This is Charles."

Charles did not speak, as if perfect stillness would render him invisible as he lay on Alex's bed.

"Sorry, I was just dropping off my books."

"No problem," said Alex as casually as if he were discussing the weather over a cup of coffee. "Before you go, there's a letter for you on your desk. I think it's from Raquel."

"Oh, thanks," Cameron said. He grabbed the letter and quickly made his way back to the door. "Nice meeting you, Charles," he said, shutting the door behind him.

Cameron walked across campus with the letter in his pocket, looking for the right place to read it. He tried sitting under one of the large oaks outside the science hall, but he could not find a comfortable position among the knotty roots. Finally he settled on a picnic bench outside the student center.

My Dearest Cameron,

Your absence is painful, but even harder to bear is your unhappiness. I suppose everything comes with a price, and there is nothing I would not have paid for our time together. I love you with the heart that you have awakened.

I so wish I could ease the concerns you expressed in your last letter, but I, like you, am not certain what the future holds. I want your days to be filled with joy. You are young, and you are good, so good, and you deserve to be happy.

No matter what happens, please know that you are constantly surrounded by my loving thoughts.

All my love,

R

Cameron folded the letter, put it back in his pocket, and walked to the nearest bar, Myrtle's Good Time Pub. During the next week, Cameron spent many hours at Myrtle's, often staying until closing, stumbling from his stool when the bartender said he could no longer stay.

It was nearly three in the morning when Cameron arrived back at his room after a particularly heavy night of drinking at Myrtle's. Alex was in bed with the lights off, but not asleep.

"Hello, room-matey," moaned Alex.

"How was your night?" asked Cameron.

"Well, I'd have to say that it would have been much better if I hadn't been beaten up."

"What do you mean?" Cameron asked.

"I think I'm in pretty bad shape."

Cameron flipped on the lights. The sight of Alex took his breath. Alex was curled into a fetal position in boxers and a T-shirt. His face and arms were covered with bruises and dried blood. There was a six-inch laceration on his thigh.

"Alex, what happened?"

"I was walking back here. I was pretty drunk. I passed these jock-head oafs. One of them was pretty cute. I guess I said something to that effect, but I wasn't even sure they heard me. Then one of the gorillas was tackling me. He started punching me in the face while the other one kicked me, saying it was queers like me that made the world all screwed up." Alex grimaced as he took a breath. "Then they stopped. I was thankful for that. I wasn't sure they would stop."

"Alex, What can I do?"

Alex didn't say anything at first. Then he cleared his throat. "I guess you could start by making the world a better place. How about that?" He tried to punctuate the sentence with forced laughter, but instead, he began to cry.

Cameron crawled behind Alex and held him gently. Doing so felt unexpectedly natural.

Alex stopped crying. "Thanks, Cameron. It really helps."

And Cameron realized that it helped ease his own pain, as well.

"God, you smell good," Alex whispered just before he drifted into sleep.

Foul Ball

R yan Rigsby knows that God has a plan for him. He feels that sometime soon, he'll know what that plan is.

"That'll be sixty-seven cents," says the girl behind the counter.

Ryan counts the coins in his palm. "I'll take a plain bagel, too," he says, passing the majority of his net worth to the girl.

Ryan takes a seat in a corner booth and begins to pray. His prayer begins as a blessing of his coffee and bagel and the upcoming sermon he will deliver on the street. The prayer then moves into a long meditation sprinkled with gentle requests that God's plan for him be more clearly revealed.

Ryan's prayers begin in the front of his brain, just behind his eyes. As a session progresses, the prayer moves to the top of his head, at which time he relaxes his neck so that bowed head drops further, allowing the prayer to move to its final position in the very rear of his skull. It is in this place, the deepest recess of his mind, where Ryan finds grace, where the chaos of the world evaporates. His fear and disappointment dissipates, and he is free. Warm. Liquid.

"Oh, shit!"

Ryan's bubble of grace bursts.

"Shit, shit, shit!" shouts a short-skirted girl to her shorter-skirted friend who giggles at a latté lake on the table. The two decide on another booth and take a seat.

Ryan is angry. He tries to return to his prayer, but gives up after several minutes of being stuck behind his eyeballs.

"Hey, Overby. What's shaking?" says Mark Crocker, wearing the lucky bowling shoes he always wears on days he's pitching. "Sorry about nearly killing us yesterday."

"You should be," Billy says with a smile.

"I'm sure glad you invited that Cameron fellow along. If it weren't for him, who knows what would have happened."

The story of the previous day's boating adventure is retold to each Wave that enters the locker room. As Gary Ashton leaps from the top of a storage cabinet in imitation of Crocker falling from the cockpit, right fielder Shaun Grissom interrupts the tenth retelling.

"Shit. That ain't nothing, man. You think you had a bad day. You oughta trade places with me. My goddamn little brother called me yesterday to tell me he's a faggot."

"Must mean you got a little pink in your blood, too," chides Crocker.

The rest of the team joins in.

"I knew you were checking me out in the shower in Detroit," says first baseman Ron Brown.

"What are you doing tonight after the game?" asks shortstop Jave Martinez. "My wife's hairdresser is looking for a date."

Grissom does not laugh. "Ain't nothing funny about this. This is my goddamn brother I'm talking about."

Leftfielder Dale Currin pats Grissom on the shoulder, "Lighten up, Griz. It could be worse."

"How could it be worse?"

"Lots of ways. What if he had called to say he had cancer?"

"I could handle that. But I can't handle being the brother of a homo."

"I hear you, Griz," says Waves catcher Chad Reynolds. "I'd disown my brother on the spot if he told me he was a

queen. And after I disowned him, I'd shoot him, unless my father got to him first."

"Christ. That's harsh," says Overby.

"Harsh nothing. You gotta live with your choices."

"So you think it's a choice?" Dale Currin asks.

Reynolds nods. "Yeah, but a damn bad one."

Currin turns to Grissom. "How about you, Griz? You think it's a choice?"

"Hell, yeah, it's a choice. And I can't stand the idea of my little brother standing hand in hand with some faggot at the pearly gates explaining his choice to the Big Man."

Currin smiles. "Well, I tell you fellows, it ain't ever been a choice for me. I've been in love with pussy as long as I can remember, and if I felt about anything else like I feel about pussy, ain't no one that could have stopped me from getting it."

"Yeah," says relief pitcher Andy Stubbs, "you guys think it's a choice, then you're a lot lighter in the loafers than I am."

"I ain't talking about a choice for me. I'm talking about my brother going off to college and deciding he's a goddamn queer."

"Yeah, it ain't a choice for me either," says Reynolds defensively. "I'd rather die than be a queer."

Currin laughs. "I'm sure that's a relief to the few anorexic, fake-blond groupies in Raleigh yet to experience your loving."

Amanda sits at her kitchen table trying not to think of Cameron. She is failing miserably.

She remembers the first time Cameron visited her in Raleigh. She had offered to go down to Wilmington and pick him up, but he had insisted on taking the bus. His bus was late, and she had waited for over two hours at the bus station, the smell of stale urine seeping from the men's room and five different men plopping into the vinyl seat beside hers, though there were several rows of empty seats. One had offered to teach her the secrets of the alien species that uses mind control to shape the events of human history; but she passed on the offer and went outside where the animal stares of a group of teenaged boys all dressed in maroon and gold chased her back inside.

She sat in a single folding chair near the ticket counter, her mind finding refuge from the fear and boredom by delving through scenes of her month-long romance with Cameron. For the previous four weeks, she had lived for the weekends. She enjoyed their days together, but more than anything, she loved their nights. Cameron approached sex in a way she had never experienced. He was simultaneously gentle and forceful. One moment he would lightly explore her thighs with his tongue, and the next he would seem to be attempting to drive his entire body inside her. One moment he would be gently swaying on top of her, barely moving inside her as he gently kissed one breast and then the other, and in a flash she would find herself on elbows and knees as he thrust like a bull into her from behind. And always, it was exactly what she wanted him to be doing.

"How do you do it?" she asked him after an evening session of lovemaking on the ocean side of Shackleford Banks.

"I listen," he said, handing her a plastic cup of chardonnay.

"To what?" She wanted to know exactly what was happening when they made love.

But he had responded only with a laugh and the single word, "Everything."

By the time Cameron's bus had arrived, Amanda had worked herself into a frenzy of desire. The other passengers seemed to be exiting the bus with deliberate

  *Full Count*

slowness; and when Cameron finally stepped off the bus, Amanda charged and wrapped herself around him with an embrace filled with desperate need. It felt wondrous to be holding him. She rubbed one palm over his chest and rested the other on top of his hips, taking an inventory of the body she had come to think of as hers. She would get him home as fast as she could. They'd make love in her bed for the first time. They'd be at it all night. She felt herself stepping back into a wonderful month-long dream.

"Amanda, I want you to meet Stella. Stella, this is Amanda."

"He's told me all about you," said the woman.

Amanda felt herself stepping back out of the dream as Cameron explained that Stella, a white-haired, heavily tattooed cross between a grandmother and a bouncer, was traveling all over the country collecting testimony from people who had spoken directly to a divine being.

"How interesting," Amanda said, making no effort to sound sincere.

"I told Stella that we'd love to buy her dinner if she'd tell us about her work."

"Is there a Waffle House nearby?" inquired Stella.

"There's one on Capital Boulevard," Amanda said as she felt the dream drift further away.

As Amanda sits in her kitchen trying not to think of Cameron, she remembers that she had ended up enjoying Stella's stories of divine contact; and the plate of scrambled eggs, hash browns, and sausage links had provided welcomed fuel when a few hours later, with Stella off on her quest for God-knowers and Cameron wrapped in the satin sheets of Amanda's bed, she had finally stepped back into her dream.

Amanda pours herself a half glass of bourbon and begins to pull Cameron's oil paintings from her walls.

Within a half hour, she has formed a small mountain of canvas oceans in her backyard.

She goes to the garage for gasoline.

After Margaret oversees the second shift at the Billy Overby Foundation Soup Kitchen, she goes home to make a very special pot of soup. Regardless of what Billy had said, she could tell he wasn't feeling up to par and a few bowls of her chicken-artichoke noodle soup are in order.

Cameron finishes mowing the back yard and, deciding the front can wait until morning, he decides it's time for a beer.

Margaret removes a pot of egg noodles from the burner, pours the noodles into a colander, runs cold water over twists of pasta, and then dumps them into a larger pot holding chicken broth, chopped carrots and celery, chunks of meat pulled from a half dozen chicken thighs, and shredded artichoke hearts. Margaret has always believed that soup is one of the best ways to nourish body and soul, bringing comfort to both the maker and consumer.

After seasoning the pot with salt, pepper, and granulated garlic, she scoops a test bowl and finds it up to her standards.

Amanda splashes gasoline around the pile of paintings and breathes in the fumes with deep breaths. She is giddy when she strikes the match and tosses it toward the paintings. Flames rush to meet the match, and within minutes, the fire is warming Amanda's cheeks.

Cameron finishes his beer and disrobes for a shower, but on his way to the bathroom he is distracted by the pictures and memorabilia on Billy's walls.

Cameron studies the pictures, tracing Billy's evolution from little leaguer to high school all-star to first round draft pick to major league batting leader. A wire hoop extends from an oak plaque to hold the first baseball Billy ever hit out of a major league park. Cameron can't resist taking the ball out of the wire hoop. He wonders what major league pitcher last held the ball before Billy swatted it over the fence.

"One away and Billy Overby comes to the plate," says Cameron in his imaginary radio announcer's voice. "The rookie's off to quite a start this year, but we'll see how he stands up against Lawrence's fastball."

Cameron kicks his leg up and throws an imaginary pitch.

"And Lawrence blows strike one right by the rookie."

Another imaginary pitch and Cameron moves ahead in the count 2-0.

"It looks like Lawrence is just too strong for the kid today."

The third imaginary pitch is a ball, low and outside, but the fourth pitch, a fastball, hangs up in the strike zone and Billy sends it toward the bleachers.

"It looks like it may be outta here, folks," says the imaginary radio announcer.

Cameron has become the imaginary centerfielder and is approaching the warning track when Margaret Overby steps through the front door with her pot of soup.

Cameron freezes, wondering what it must be like to encounter a naked stranger playing imaginary baseball.

"Hello, son, I'm Margaret Overby. I'm just dropping off a bowl of soup for Billy. I didn't expect anybody to be home."

"Hi. I'm Cameron Lawrence. I'm a friend of Billy's," Cameron says, using the baseball in a futile attempt to cover himself.

"Well, don't mind me. Just put this in the refrigerator when you get a chance," Margaret says, setting the pot on the end table nearest the door. "Nice to meet you, Cameron."

"Very nice to meet you, Mrs. Overby."

"Call me Margaret, dear. A friend of Billy's is a friend of mine."

The door closes and Cameron collapses to the floor in embarrassment as he watches the ball sail over the imaginary fence.

Amanda stares into the fire, thinking of all the memories she hopes to burn away.

Cameron showers, grabs a beer, and turns on the television in time to see Billy's first trip to the plate.

Margaret, still smiling over her encounter with Cameron, sips hot chocolate and sends loving thoughts to Billy through the television screen. There he is, her boy. She studies the strong forearms given to him by his father. And when the camera zooms in on his face, she thinks how his pale gray eyes are also a paternal gift. In his lips and brow she finds her own features, features that had originally belonged to her own father. She thinks how she created the marvelous creature in front of her, the most marvelous creature she could ever imagine. It is a thought she has had many thousands of times, but a thought of which she never tires.

As Billy steps into the box against Cincinnati pitcher Brett Lancaster, he realizes that something is horribly wrong. He has positioned his right foot in the box and twisted it back and forth three times. He has shouldered his bat and brought his left foot into the box. By this

point, all thoughts are supposed to have fled his mind. But as Lancaster stares toward the plate, Billy finds himself thinking of Cameron. Lancaster goes into his windup and delivers the first pitch high and away. Ball one.

Billy steps out of the box and tries to shake Cameron out of his mind.

Amanda sips a gin and tonic and watches her fire burn slowly out.

Lancaster's second pitch splits the middle of the plate a few inches above Billy's waist. Billy could not ask for a more perfect pitch. It's a pitch that he'd normally rip on a line to left field, possibly for extra bases. But by the time Billy recognizes the beautiful possibilities the pitch has to offer, the umpire is signaling a strike.

Margaret Overby is surprised that her son took the pitch, but when the play-by-play announcer proclaims the same surprise, she mutters, "Oh, what do you know, you big buffoon."

Margaret watches Billy step out of the batter's box, take a half swing, touch the brim of his cap with his left hand, take another practice swing, touch the brim of his cap with his right hand.

And then she sees something that fills her with alarm. Billy takes another practice swing.

Billy Overby cannot believe what he has just done. For as long as he can remember, he has performed the same ritual between pitches. In sixth grade, Billy faced the thirteen-year-old phenom Gerrard Burrows in the final inning of the regional Little League championship; and it was the perfect performance of the ritual, its symmetry, its simplicity, that led Billy to what he has always thought of as "the clear zone," a gift from the baseball gods. In the clear zone, batting is a simple task, a simple matter of letting the primitive regions of the mind do what they deem best. But outside of the clear zone, the frontal lobe, the curse of consciousness, takes over, and an insurmountable wall of thought stands between the batter and a base hit. With the extra swing Billy has angered the gods, and they have banished him from the clear zone.

Billy tries to pray to Bob, but it is suddenly obvious to him that God's name is not Bob, after all.

Amanda touches the marshmallow she has roasted over the coals of Cameron's paintings. The marshmallow's skin is crisp, just shy of charred. Perfect. She removes the marshmallow from the end of the sharpened elm branch and places it atop the chocolate squares resting on her graham cracker. Taking a bite, Amanda feels the warm chocolate smear on her upper lip, and she knows she is going to be fine.

Not knowing what else to do, Billy steps back into the batter's box. He is dizzy, floating on a sea of thousands of spectators and the noise they are producing. The statistic four-point-seven-three, Lancaster's earned run average, flashes across Billy's mind, and on top of it all remains a ghost-like image of Cameron. As Billy twists his right foot into the batter's box, he nearly stumbles. He tries to relax as he inhales deeply and shoulders the bat, but as he exhales it is confidence, not anxiety that exits his body. As he places his left foot in the batter's box, he knows he is totally unprepared to face the next pitch.

Amanda stabs the tip of her stick though another marshmallow.

Billy decides to take the next pitch, and as soon as he makes this decision, his mind begins to question baseball's odd use of "take." Why does "taking" a pitch mean not swinging at it? For years, Billy's mind has quietly accepted baseball's twist on the term without affording it a second thought, but now his mind is aggressively curious. He tries to shove the question into the recesses of his cerebellum, but it pops right back out.

While half of Billy's mind notes that he is now behind in the count, the other half is riding the following train of thought:

Wouldn't it be fun to run the bases backwards? What would happen if I decided to kneel down in the batter's box? Or what if I strike out and run to first anyway? And what if God's name really is Bob, and what if He comes down and asks me to tell the entire stadium that He wants to add a new commandment? And finally: Damn, what is it about the way that Cameron guy smells?

Lancaster fires another pitch down the middle, and it goes untouched for strike two.

Billy's mind is certainly not the first in baseball to stray outside the lines. Rube Waddell, a strikeout leader seven times between 1900 and 1907, regularly disrupted games when he sprinted from the mound to chase fire engines. Mark "The Bird" Fidrych, who made love to his girlfriend on the pitcher's mound the day he was called to the major leagues, spent several minutes of every game talking to the baseball and crawling on his hands and knees as he groomed the infield. And minor league manager Frank Peters sometimes pondered the possibility of rotating his nine starters every inning so that each played every position during the course of the game. On August 31, 1974, he put the idea into practice, and the result was an 8-7 victory.

Billy does not share Frank Peters' good fortune. Lancaster's next pitch is a slider almost a foot outside the plate, but Billy finds himself whiffing at the air for strike three.

A few innings later, Billy has managed to subdue his rampant thoughts, at least partially, and when he comes to the plate with Dale Currin on first and no outs, he is able to lay a bunt down the first-base line, despite the fact that it occurs to him that this would be an ideal time to run the bases clockwise.

In the seventh inning he manages to draw a walk, due primarily to the fact that Lancaster runs out of steam and throws three consecutive pitches in the dirt.

In the bottom of the ninth, Billy comes to the plate for what will be one of the most bizarre at-bats of his career.

With two outs, Gary Ashton stands on third, representing the winning run. Cincinnati relief pitcher Denny Wright, all six and a half feet and three hundred pounds of him, is a daunting figure on the mound, but Billy manages to relax enough to consider the possibility of putting the ball into play.

Billy watches Wright's first pitch, a curve ball, catch the corner for strike one. Billy makes good contact with the next pitch, sending it over the right field fence, but it drifts just outside the foul pole. Strike two.

The next pitch is another curve, low and away. Billy lunges to protect the plate but misses. However, as catcher Tony Shriver pulls the ball out of the dirt, Phillip Sexton, the umpire and the only person on the field who comes close to matching the physical stature of Denny Wright, signals foul tip. Everyone in the park, other than Phillip Sexton, knows Billy has just struck out, but baseball is not a democracy, and the count remains no balls and two strikes. When the pitch is replayed in slow motion on the

large screen above the scoreboard, thousands of Waves fans pretend to see the foul tip.

Denny Wright is furious, and with three balls to spare, he decides to unleash his ire on Overby. Wright rocks his large frame into one of the slowest wind-ups in the league, lifts his monstrous left leg almost neck high, and fires a fastball at Billy's head.

Billy ducks, sparing his head the hundred mile an hour collision with rock-hard cowhide; but the intended bean ball, after passing above Billy's hunched body, strikes part of the eight inches or so of bat positioned above Billy's right shoulder.

The ball then flies back over Billy's body and rolls slowly towards third base in fair territory.

Billy opens his eyes, and seeing the ball in play, runs safely to first as Ashton slides under Shriver's tag at home, giving the Waves the victory on an accidental squeeze play.

The post-strikeout infield hit, combined with the earlier strikeout, walk, and sacrifice, leaves Billy one for two for the night, raising his average closer to four hundred.

That night, Billy and Cameron laugh as they recount Billy's over-the-back single, but they laugh much harder as Cameron tells Billy about his nude encounter with Margaret.

As they laugh, Billy's earlier confusion seems to disappear, and he feels happier than he has in years.

For the next two games, Billy manages to get by at the plate, despite not being able to get back into his regular routine, and for the next two nights he spends pleasurable post-game hours with Cameron. Even when Cameron speaks of his romantic involvements with other men, it never occurs to Billy that he may be developing a crush on his houseguest.

It won't be until he leaves for the Waves' road series against Pittsburgh that Billy will realize things might be getting a bit complicated.

In 1948, seventeen-year-old Ruth Ann Steinhagen became infatuated with Cubs first baseman Eddie Waitkus. The young woman went to sleep each night at the foot of the collection of photos and candles that composed her Eddie Waitkus shrine, and all was well with her unrequited romance until it was announced that Waitkus was to be traded to Philadelphia at the completion of the 1948 season. Ms. Steinhagen was disconsolate and refused to passively accept the idea of losing her love to a rival town.

When Waitkus visited Chicago with the Philidelphia squad the following season, Steinhagen lured him into a room at the Edgewater Beach Hotel where she waited for him with a rifle. When Waitkus entered the room, Ms. Steinhagen fired without a word.

In the end, Waitkus recovered and went on to one of the best seasons of his career in 1950. Though Ms. Steinhagen spent three years in a mental hospital following the attack, she claimed she never felt as much joy as when she opened fire on her traitorous lover.

It is likely that Ruth Ann Steinhagen's obsession with Eddie Waitkus could be blamed, at least partially, on phenylethylamine. Phenylethylamine is a potent amphetamine that the human brain has been producing for thousands of years. Millennia ago, out on the African plain, when one of our ancestors found another of our ancestors physically attractive, the brain would start full-scale production of phenylethylamine, and before long what had begun as a simple appreciation would be transformed, literally, into an addiction. We are a species that thrives, in a large part, thanks to the millions of phenylethylamine addicts who have walked the planet.

If you want to see phenylethylamine in action, go to the nearest coffee shop and look for the two young poets in love, or go to the park and look for the two forty-somethings sipping gin out of plastic cups and making out like prom dates.

Or take a look at Billy Overby, one of phenylethylamine's most recent addicts. Billy, staring out of the small, cloud-filled window of the team's chartered jet, thinks of Cameron. He wonders if Cameron is painting. Or maybe he's working in the yard. Or maybe enjoying a beer on the patio.

Billy tries to will the plane to make a u-turn, but it refuses to cease its journey towards Pittsburgh, away from the source of Billy's addiction.

In Raleigh, Cameron watches the local news and considers calling Amanda.

Amanda is on her bedroom floor. She is supposed to be moving from Cobra to Downward Facing Dog, but her new yoga video has been unable to deliver the tranquility promised by its cover; and Amanda decides she cannot possibly find personal enlightenment until she has her period, which is now three long days late.

A ringing phone interrupts a very un-yoga-like groan of despair.

"Hello."

Nothing.

"Hello?"

Nothing.

"Hello."

Amanda is about to hang up the phone when a familiar sigh comes over the line.

"Cameron, is that you?"

If she has gained any placidity during her failed yoga session, it has vanished. Her muscles tense and her chest tightens.

"Cameron, I've been thinking about you. I want you to know I feel awful about shooting *Sam I Am*. How's she doing?"

While Cameron explains that the blows Amanda inflicted upon *Sam I Am* were fatal, Amanda thinks about the period she's not having.

"Your paintings? Well, yeah, I'd like to talk to you about your paintings. Maybe we could get together for a cup of coffee. Are you in Wilmington?"

Amanda cannot believe Cameron's response.

"How long have you been in Raleigh?"

Amanda looks at her Caller ID: Overby, William.

"Damn it, Cameron! You were never in Raleigh more than three straight days the entire time we were dating!"

Amanda's guilt over having destroyed Cameron's boat and his paintings is being chased away by anger.

"You've been in town almost a week and haven't called. I guess you've been too occupied with Mr. Baseball Hero."

Cameron's claim that he was scared to call her angers Amanda even more. She remembers the day she had sold her first million-dollar home. The buyer had almost walked when she had refused to explore the master bathroom's Jacuzzi with him. When she had told Cameron, he had called the buyer and threatened to personally remove his testicles if he caused Amanda another uncomfortable moment.

"Scared? Cameron, you are a lot of things, but scared isn't one of them. I bet if I could hit a homerun you wouldn't have been scared to call me. You want your paintings? Meet me tonight at seven at Foster's."

Amanda slams the receiver back onto its cradle, and

then goes into the backyard with a shovel and box to collect the remains of Cameron's paintings.

In Pittsburgh, Billy had entered his hotel room and fallen into a three-hour nap, which is now being interrupted.

"Wake up, sleepyhead. It's poker time," announces his roommate Mark Crocker, who is followed by Gary Ashton carrying a case of beer and a deck of cards, and Shaun Grissom who is loaded down with chips, salsa, a bag of pretzels, and a large jar of mustard.

"I'm feeling lucky, boys," warns Grissom as he dumps his junk food on the bureau.

As seven o'clock moves closer, Cameron grows more nervous. He is amazed at Amanda's ability to stay angry at him. He understands that his refusal to live inland was a constant source of frustration for Amanda, but he had genuinely cared for her, still genuinely cares for her. And damn it, she killed his home.

The poker game has been in progress for a little over an hour when Dale Currin joins in. Billy cares little that he has lost seventy-six dollars because thoughts of Cameron have kept his mind pleasantly occupied; but then Dale Currin, dealing a hand of five-card draw—deuces and the suicide king wild—turns to Shaun Grissom and asks how his brother is doing.

"Shit, Currin," says Mark Crocker, tossing three dollars in the pot. "You know Griz doesn't want to talk about his faggot brother in the middle of a card game."

The word "faggot" rings in Billy's skull. For days he has thought of little other than Cameron, but it has not crossed his mind that he might be gay, that his infatuation, his obsession, might be of a sexual nature.

Shaun Grissom sees the three dollars and raises the bet

another two bucks. "I talked to Ronnie last night. I told him, look man, you're my little brother and that ain't ever gonna change. I told him I didn't ever want to meet his little friend, or talk about his little friend, but that I wanted him to be happy."

"What did he say to that?" asks Gary Ashton through a mouthful of chips.

"He said that his little friend was bigger than me and made almost as much money. And I said, 'Didn't I just say I didn't want to hear about your little friend?' and then I told him I loved him and hung up."

"You're dealing with it better than I would," says Crocker as he requests two new cards.

"What about you, Overby?" asks Dale Currin.

"Me. I don't know. Two guys, that's kind of different, I guess."

"I'm talking about cards. How many you want?"

"Oh. I'll take two."

Billy picks up his cards and studies his hand. A pair of jacks.

As Cameron sits in the courtyard of Foster's, his eyes are wide open, like an animal of prey. He replays Amanda's assault of *Sam I Am* and wonders if she's somewhere on the perimeter, plotting another act of vengeance; but just when his paranoia starts to pick up momentum, Amanda appears at the table bearing a gift-wrapped box.

Everyone has dropped out of the hand except for Billy and Crocker. Billy knows that it's unlikely that a pair of jacks will beat whatever Crocker's holding, but he has decided to bluff, raising Crocker's every raise. Worst case, he'll win the pot. Best case, he'll lose his last dollar bill and excuse himself from the game so that he can get the fresh air he craves.

......

"You look great," says Cameron, interrupting another awkward silence.

"You sound surprised."

"I think I am no longer capable of being surprised."

"Is that right?"

"See that man in the seersucker suit?"

"I see him."

"If he were to spontaneously combust, not only would I not be surprised, I would be certain that it was somehow my fault."

"Jesus, Cameron, that's pathetic."

"Yes, it is. I feel more pathetic than I've ever felt."

"Well, stop it."

"I wish it were that easy."

"Christ, Overby, you bet over a hundred bucks on a pair of jacks."

"I guess I didn't bluff very well."

"You bluffed just fine," says Crocker, raking the night's largest pot across the table as Billy excuses himself from the game.

Outside, the Pittsburgh night is cool against Billy's face. A pair of large, dark sunglasses hides much of his face, allowing him to walk the city's streets in anonymity.

"Cameron, I really am sorry about the boat. I want you to tell me how much it will cost to replace," Amanda says, pulling her checkbook from her purse.

"I don't know."

"Of course you know. How much did you pay for it?"

"About twelve grand."

"That sounds fair." Amanda begins to write out a check.

"I don't want you to do that."

"I didn't ask, did I?" Amanda finishes writing the check and places it in front of Cameron.

Cameron picks up the check and rips it in two.

"What are you doing?"

Cameron places the two halves of the check together and rips them again. "I said I didn't want it."

"But it's only right."

"What would have been right is for you not to have shot my boat. But you did. But I know that you shot it because of the way I made you feel. And you couldn't shoot me. So you shot my boat because of the way I made you feel. Who's to say whose fault it was?"

"I pulled the trigger."

"Because I made you."

"I pulled the trigger because I wanted to."

"You wanted to because of the way I made you feel."

"Jesus, Cameron. You're not God. I shot your stupid boat because sometimes I get crazy, and this particular time I got crazy, I got my gun."

"But I made you crazy."

"You're making me crazy right now."

"See?"

"I'm paying you for the boat."

"I won't let you. I just want my paintings."

The waitress brings their cocktails, and Amanda takes a long sip of her gin and tonic. "What if I told you that I sold them all?" She removes the box of ashes from the table and places it by her feet.

On one hand, Billy's sure that he cannot fathom having sex with a man. On the other hand, he sure wishes he could spend time with Cameron, could talk with him, could smell him; and if he's being completely honest with himself, he wouldn't mind swapping back rubs.

. . . . . .

"He's from Atlanta. And he only has one arm."

"He only has one arm?" Cameron asks incredulously.

"He lost the other as a child. On a safari with his father. A run-in with a rhino. He told me the whole story," explains Amanda.

"But I thought you said he used to be a professional golfer."

"Yes, that's right."

"A one-armed golfer?"

"Incredible, isn't it?"

"I want my paintings, Amanda, even if you have to buy them back from the independently wealthy, one-armed, rhino-hunting golfer from Atlanta.

"You really want them?"

"As soon as possible. We're just not good for each other, and the sooner we're out of each other's lives, the better off we'll be."

Amanda lifts the box and rips the paper away. "Take your stupid paintings, you bastard." She dumps the ashes over Cameron's head, composes herself, and walks out, trying not to think of her still absent period.

Billy stops at a pay phone and calls his mother.

"Hey, Mom. Can I ask you a question?"

"Well, of course, dear."

"What was it like when you and Dad first met?"

"What do you mean, dear?'

"Did you fall in love?"

"Oh, honey, I fell in love as hard and as fast as anyone ever has."

"What was that like?"

"It was the scariest, most wonderful time of my life."

On Monday, April 9, 1965, at seven in the evening, Margaret was stirring a large vat of soup above a small fire in the small yard of her small house in Louisville, Kentucky. Three men sat on Margaret's stoop and sipped soup. The men were regulars at Margaret's, where every Monday and Thursday, anyone who wanted could have two free servings of soup.

Another man crossed the street and stopped beside the large, iron vat.

"You need a bowl," Margaret informed the newcomer. She directed his attention to the hand-painted sign staked in the yard:

BRING YOUR OWN BOWL
NO DRINKING

For over three years, Margaret had spent Monday and Thursday afternoons feeding Louisville's most unfortunate. Eddie Wister, the local butcher, set aside beef bones throughout the week for stock and sold her pounds of stew beef at a generous discount. Mr. Larson, the owner of Larson's Groceries and Produce, provided the carrots, celery, tomatoes, potatoes, canned corn, and salt and pepper at cost. Margaret's soup might have offered little in the way of culinary fireworks, but Mr. Stewart, the first recipient of Margaret's free soup and one of the regulars sitting on the stoop, said that Margaret added doses of love to her soup that made it better than anything he'd ever eaten, including all the fancy meals he'd had in Paris, which he claimed to have visited regularly before he fell on hard times, a turn of events which changed from telling to telling.

"I don't care for any soup, thank you."

"Well, I'm afraid that's all I have to offer," Margaret said, fully aware that the starch-shirted, well-groomed man was looking for something other than food.

"Maybe I could help you."

"That's very kind of you, sir, but maybe you could tell

me just what leads you to think I need help."

A van, hand-painted with a variety of pastel flowers, pulled up to the curb. A half dozen young people, all with hair to their waists, emptied out into the yard as the stranger in the crisp white shirt explained that he was in town to open a sporting goods store. His eyes were bright and never moved from Margaret as he explained the intricacies of breaking into the sporting goods market.

"That's all very interesting. Now if you'll excuse me, I'm a bit busy," she said, pleased to see the confidence drop from the stranger's face as she turned to serve the young hippies holding less than masterfully-turned, handmade bowls glazed in floral designs similar to that of the van.

"Okay, maybe I'll see you around," said the stranger, turning to leave.

"Maybe so," Margaret said, studying his sturdy, broad-shouldered frame out of the corner of her eyes as she ladled soup for Jasmine Love, the hippie name Joan and Bud Salter's girl had taken when she traded the Methodist youth choir for less traditional spiritual pursuits.

When Margaret woke up the next morning, she was alarmed that images of the stranger, which had kept her awake hours past her eleven o'clock bedtime, were still with her.

She dressed, breakfasted, and walked the seven blocks to St. Mary's Hospital where she was the director of the volunteer program. She tried to banish all thoughts of the stranger, but in the end had to work an extra half hour and still accomplished very little due to her distracted mind.

Thursday afternoon came, and as Margaret diced the carrots and celery, she wondered if the stranger might stop by again. She had never had such immediate feelings for a man, but she explained to herself that her infatuation was really an illusion, made possible only by her complete lack of knowledge of the stranger.

As a child, her father – who was fascinated by people and liked to study them from a comfortable distance – was fond of reminding her that familiarity breeds contempt. As Margaret chopped the last of the celery, she thought of her father and told herself that the stranger was just another person, one more member of a self-serving, power-hungry species, much more prone to destruction than love. Still, she hoped to see him again.

It was a very busy soup night. Margaret had served over forty people, and the sky was darkening when the stranger showed up.

"I brought a bowl," he said.

"You have, indeed."

The stranger said nothing as Margaret made several passes across the bottom of the vat to produce another serving. When his bowl was half full, the stranger thanked Margaret and took a seat on the stoop.

Margaret busied herself by going inside for more vegetables and stock. As she replenished the vat, she concentrated on ignoring the stranger who sat on the top step of her stoop, silently surveying her yard and the surrounding houses.

By the time the fire beneath the vat was reduced to a few smoldering coals glowing in the dark, Margaret's regulars had made their way back out into the world, but the stranger remained on her stoop.

"Haven't you finished that bowl, yet?"

"I'm a fairly slow eater," said the stranger.

"No, you're a very slow eater."

"It depends on the setting."

"And how would you describe this setting?"

"Well, it's a beautiful evening. A bit cool, but that's how I like it. A pleasant lawn. And listen," the stranger said,

shutting his eyes and raising a finger toward the sky. "The sounds of the city are drifting down upon us. Do you hear them?"

"I hear them," Margaret said. "Nothing like the tranquil sound of traffic."

The stranger ignored Margaret's sarcasm. "But that's not the best part."

"What's the best part?"

"I'm talking to the most beautiful woman I've ever met."

"You're too much."

"And you're just right."

Margaret spent the first part of that night learning everything she could about William Overby's life, and the second half learning about his body.

Months passed before Margaret could think of anything that didn't pertain to William.

Billy Overby hangs up the phone and walks for several more miles. That night he dreams of swimming with Cameron in a giant bowl of soup.

Seventh Inning Stretch

Cameron wakes, but an iron blanket of depression lies atop him. Maybe I'll stay in bed today, he thinks.

Amanda wakes with her hand on her belly. During the night she dreamt that she was pregnant, not with Cameron's child, but a small panda bear. That would be nice, thinks Amanda as she moves fully into consciousness. If I have to be pregnant, a pet panda bear would be perfect.

Ryan Rigsby awakes filled with the fire of God. He springs from the bed and dresses. "ALMIGHTY LORD, I AM YOUR VESSEL. USE ME TODAY AS YOU SEE FIT," he says as he pulls a blue-striped athletic sock over his calf. He throws on his jeans and slides his feet into a pair of worn sandals and then joins his parents in the kitchen for breakfast.

"Good morning, Ryan," his mother says, pouring Ryan a bowl of cornflakes.

"You going to find a job today, son?" his father asks from behind his newspaper.

"I AM BLESSED, FATHER, FOR I WORK FOR THE GREATEST BOSS OF ALL."

Paul Rigsby lets his paper drop to the table. "You better tell that boss man of yours he needs to start paying you. Your mother and I weren't put on this earth to baby-sit a grown man."

"FOR JOHN THE BAPTIST CAME, NEITHER EATING BREAD NOR DRINKING WINE; AND YE SAY, HE HATH A DEVIL. LUKE SEVEN, THIRTY-THREE."

"And if you don't get yourself a job, thou, too, shall find yourself living in the wilderness. The Book of Paul

Rigsby, chapter one, verse one," responds Ryan's father before going back behind his paper.

Cameron remains in bed and lets his mind drift. He thinks of Molly Desmond, a college friend who had introduced him to painting. Molly painted unauthorized murals on the walls of campus buildings.

"Won't you get in trouble if you get caught?" Cameron had asked her once.

"I don't know. Maybe you could look up the penalty for beautification in the student handbook. Besides, who would catch me? I set up. I do my work. Sometimes crowds gather, but, you see, because I'm doing something I think I should be doing, they think I'm doing something I should be doing. Like most things, it's all about attitude."

One night, Cameron was walking across campus after a long night in the library when he came across Molly working under the dim courtyard lights outside a freshman girl's dormitory. She was painting a giant aquarium in which swam mermaids and tropical fish. Two of the mermaids appeared to be making love on the pebble covered floor.

"Hey, Molly. You're working late."

"I'm going to the lake with Yvonne this weekend. I want to finish before we leave."

"Things going well with Yvonne?"

"We're doing as well as can be expected for two beautiful, intelligent women who love each other. How about you?"

"I guess things are fine. A certain level of unidentified malaise, but nothing out of the norm."

Molly brushed auburn locks onto one of the mermaids. "Yvonne says that the best remedy for the blues is nudity. She says depression is simply a failure to appreciate the ridiculous."

"I'll try it some time."

"Why not now? Come on, I'll join you."

Before Cameron could respond, Molly had slipped the straps of her denim dress over her shoulders and let it fall to the ground, revealing her healthily plump body, her black panties dividing the fair skin of her belly and thighs. She grabbed a paint-covered sheet and danced with it across the courtyard.

Cameron felt obliged to join in. He took off his shoes and stripped, then grabbed Molly's dress from the ground and twirled it in the night air as he chased Molly's laughter through the courtyard. Two drunk frat guys were the first to join in, and within minutes the courtyard was filled with dozens of students in varying degrees of nudity.

After the dance, Cameron helped Molly finish the mermaid mural. "How's your malaise?" she asked.

Cameron smiled and brushed a dorsal fin onto a parrotfish, "You know, it seems to have lifted just a little."

Cameron decides to get out of bed and go buy a canvas and some oils.

Amanda decides to go to the drugstore to buy a pregnancy test.

Ryan Rigsby decides to stop walking and start preaching. He is on Hillsborough Street across from the state university. College students and young professionals pass by as he sets his backpack on a nearby bench, inhales, and lets forth with Godly praise.

"LISTEN SINNERS—AND BROTHERS AND SISTERS, WE ARE SINNERS ALL—LISTEN NOW NOT WITH YOUR EARS BUT WITH THE LIMITLESS HEARTS THAT GOD HAS PROVIDED FOR YOU. HIS IS A MESSAGE OF LOVE AND IT IS A MESSAGE OF WARNING. THE END IS NEAR."

Ryan feels the adrenaline pumping through his body. A grin spreads across his face.

"THE END IS NEAR, BROTHERS AND SISTERS, AND FEW OF GOD'S CHILDREN ARE PREPARED. DO NOT ALLOW YOURSELF TO BE SWALLOWED BY THE BEAST. THE TRUE WAY IS STRAIGHT AND NARROW, BUT SHALL YOU WALK IT, YOUR HEART WILL BE FILLED WITH HIS GLORY."

A very pierced, very blonde young woman walking with a group of other very pierced, very blonde young women pinches Ryan's waist as she passes. The group breaks into laughter.

Amanda stands in front of a shelf filled with pregnancy tests, each claiming to be the easiest and the fastest, so she chooses by color, deciding on a pink box.

At Saunders Art Supplies, Cameron is choosing colors of his own. He arrives at the cash register with paints, brushes, canvases, and an easel that bring him over two hundred dollars closer to being completely broke, but he feels almost giddy as he leaves the store.

Ryan Rigsby has worked himself into a sweat.

"MEN'S HEARTS ARE FAILING THEM FOR FEAR AND FOR LOOKING AFTER THOSE THINGS WHICH ARE COMING ON THE EARTH: FOR THE POWERS OF HEAVEN SHALL BE SHAKEN AND THEN SHALL THEY SEE THE SON OF MAN COMING IN A CLOUD WITH POWER AND ..."

A partially filled can of diet soda exits a passing Ford Escort and strikes Ryan in the brow, briefly interrupting the twenty-seventh verse of the twenty-first chapter of St. Luke.

"...GREAT GLORY," continues Ryan, trying not to

be discouraged by the abundance of infidels in his midst.

On the patio, Cameron stares at a blank canvas.

In her bathroom, Amanda stares at the end of a plastic stick covered with her urine.

On Hillsborough Street, Ryan has decided to stand on the nearby bench to gain a positional advantage over the sinners.

Cameron squirts a glob of cadmium green on the new palette. Beside it he squirts Indian yellow, followed by rich gold, and raw sienna.

He dips the tip of a medium round brush in the raw sienna and makes a long stroke across the canvas.

A red line forms in the control window of Amanda's test stick. Her knees shake. Her heart races. In the results window sits a bright red cross. Positive. Pregnant. She goes to the living room and collapses on the couch.

"HOW PRECIOUS ALSO ARE THY THOUGHTS UNTO ME, O GOD! HOW GREAT IS THE SUM OF THEM! IF I COUNT THEM, THEY ARE MORE IN NUMBER THAN THE GRAINS OF SAND. WHEN I AWAKE, I AM STILL WITH THEE. SURELY THOU WILL SLAY THE WICKED, O GOD. DEPART FROM ME, THEREFORE, YE BLOODY MEN."

A teen on a skateboard grabs the backpack from between Ryan's legs. Ryan leaps from the bench in pursuit. The boy is almost within reach when he hurls the backpack into the street.

Ryan leaps into the street to recover his sermon-filled notebooks. He has them safe in hand when he is struck by a 1953 Cadillac driven by the bass player of a local garage band, The Holy Zinc Bolts.

Billy watches Stew Henderson's first pitch go by for a first strike. He steps out of the batter's box and tries not to wonder whether or not Cameron is watching the game.

Gary Ashton, who led off the game with a single to right, now stands on second, thanks to Dale Currin having reached base on a walk. Currin and Ashton both see first base coach Derrick Mudd give the bunt signal, but occupied with his efforts not to think of Cameron, Billy misses the sign and steps back up to the plate prepared to swing away.

Thinking that Billy might be bunting, Henderson fires a high fastball and lets his momentum carry his body toward the plate, prepared to field anything that comes his way.

Something does, indeed, come his way, but it's no bunt. Billy, putting all of his confusion and frustration into his swing, has made solid contact with the pitch, sending the ball hurtling towards Henderson's forehead. Unable to raise his glove fast enough, Henderson stops the ball with nothing but his skull, and his body drops to the ground.

While a physician attends to Stew Henderson's forehead, Derrick Mudd slaps Billy on the rear and tells him to let someone know the next time he's going to ignore a sign. Billy laughs, having no idea what Mudd is talking about.

Ryan Rigsby watches the game from his hospital room. His right leg is in a full cast, but his notebooks of sermons lay beside him unharmed.

"THEY HAVE GAPED UPON ME WITH THEIR MOUTH; THEY HAVE SMITTEN ME UPON THE CHEEK REPROACHFULLY; THEY HAVE

GATHERED THEMSELVES TOGETHER AGAINST ME."

"I'm sorry to hear that, dear," says Misty Edwards, a motherly nurse with a maternal voice and disposition. "This shot should ease the pain."

"HOLD YOUR PEACE, LET ME ALONE THAT I MAY SPEAK, AND LET COME ON ME WHAT WILL."

The morphine soon eases Ryan out of recitations of Job and into a dream of the disciples playing a game of baseball against a local team from Gagarenes. Legion, rid of his devils, is pitching a two-hitter against Jesus and crew, but Andrew doubles into left field to give the Zebedee brothers—John's at the plate and James is on deck—a chance to break the shutout.

Margaret and Cameron watch the game at Margaret's house over a meal of baked ham, butter beans, and French bread, all leftovers from the Overby Foundation Soup Kitchen.

"How many people did you serve today?" Cameron asks.

"Right at two hundred," Margaret says.

"Make it two hundred and one. I really appreciate your having me over. You and Billy have been very kind."

Margaret passes Cameron the butter. "And you saved my son's life. I'd say that makes our fortune mutual. Good people should be good to each other."

"I'm not sure I'd consider myself all that good of a person."

"And why not?"

"Oh, I don't know. I mean I try not to hurt other people if I can help it, but mostly I look after myself."

"And looking after yourself is a bad thing?"

"No, but look at you. Hundreds of people aren't hungry

right now, thanks to you."

"And that makes me feel good, so maybe I'm doing it for myself as much as for them."

"Well, I only wish my selfishness helped other people as much as yours does."

"Maybe it does. It did the other day when Mark Crocker tried to drown you all," Margaret says as Pittsburgh shortstop Jeff Weinke hits a hard grounder down the third-base line. Billy makes a diving grab and throws the ball across the diamond from his knees, beating Weinke by a half step for the third out of the inning.

"He's incredible," says Cameron.

Margaret smiles. "He certainly is. But something's been bothering him lately and I wish I knew what it is."

"Maybe it's just all the attention over the four hundred mark and everything."

"No, it's bigger than that."

"Like what?"

"I think he's in love."

"With whom?"

Margaret's smile broadens. "I have no idea."

After dinner Margaret and Billy move to the living room to watch the rest of the game. Billy strikes out during his second and third at-bats, flies out his fourth, and during his fifth trip to the plate he goes down in the count no balls, and two strikes.

Pittsburgh relief pitcher Dustin Banes throws the next pitch inside and Billy has to step back to avoid being hit. Billy inhales, taking in a breath filled with air off the Allegheny River that has drifted down rows of seats, picking up hints of beer, popcorn, hotdogs, and the pheromones of thousands of fans. Billy thinks of how calmly Cameron had steered *Screwball III* to safety. Taking another breath, he thinks how majestic Cameron had been as he stood in the

gale-force winds.

Billy steps into the box and watches the third strike pass by.

Billy finishes the game one for five, the Waves lose by a score of five runs to three, but Billy's main thought in the locker room as he is hounded by a sea of statistic-shouting reporters is that he is now only two days away from seeing Cameron again.

Amanda pictures a golden-haired little girl playing in a large backyard. Maybe the child blows bubbles into a light breeze, or maybe she giggles as a golden retriever playfully licks her face. On the edge of the vision, Amanda plants marigolds, or maybe zinnias. The girl comes over to help, squatting on chubby little legs to scrape at dirt with Amanda's hand trowel.

It is a happy, beautiful vision, one that seems ready to come true, until the child turns to the house and calls "Da-da." Amanda follows the child's gaze until she sees Cameron exit the house in jean shorts and an old tee shirt. He runs over and buries them both in his arms, but Amanda takes a whiff and, drawing none of Cameron's scent, knows it is a silly dream.

During the next days, Ryan Rigsby recuperates in the hospital, Billy Overby continues to struggle at the plate, Cameron completes a painting of the trees in Billy's backyard, and Amanda picks up the phone to call Cameron seventy-two times.

When Billy walks through his front door, worn out from a day of baseball and travel, he is greeted by a flash. And another. And another.

"That should do it," says Cameron, placing his camera on the coffee table. "I thought I'd paint a portrait of the world's greatest batter."

"Then you don't need pictures of me."

"Pretty tough series, huh?"

"I guess you could say that."

Billy goes to the kitchen for a soda. Cameron notices a slight limp.

"You got banged up a little today, didn't you?"

Todd Beecham had buried his spikes into Billy's thigh in the second inning during a close play at third. In the seventh Billy reached base when he was struck by a pitch, and two batters later he got the short end of a collision with the opposing catcher when Jave Martinez doubled.

"I guess that's why I get paid the big bucks," Billy says, popping the top off a bottle of root beer.

"I give a pretty mean massage, if you think it might help."

Billy is terrified by the offer. "Okay, if you don't mind. That would be great." Billy tries to take a sip of root beer, but coughs violently as the root beer heads down his windpipe.

Cameron walks into the dining area with a comforter from the couch. He folds the comforter in half and places it on the dining table. "There, that should make a pretty good massage table. Why don't you take off your jeans and hop up."

As Cameron kneads the muscles of his neck, Billy tries to relax, but his heart refuses to stop racing.

While Cameron pays attention to Billy's aches and pains, Mark Crocker and Gary Ashton pay attention to the women of the Golden Ladies Gentlemen's Club. Amber dances on stage as AC/DC blasts through the club.

"What the hell's gotten into Overby?" shouts Crocker over the music.

Ashton takes a slurp of his jumbo margarita. "Maybe

  *Full Count*

something shook loose while you were trying to drown us last week."

"That was some kind of fun, wasn't it?"

"Not the kind I want to have again anytime soon."

"Ah, don't be a baby," chides Crocker.

A young woman who appears to be in the middle of a month-long fast takes the stage. Amber descends and takes a seat with Ashton and Crocker.

Billy has given in to Cameron's hands and he feels more relaxed than he has in several days.

Unfortunately, as Cameron works on the muscles of his upper thigh, Billy's relaxation gives way to pleasure and he is dismayed to feel himself becoming aroused.

"That was wonderful," says Billy, snatching his jeans from the end of the table and shielding his mid-section, "but I just remembered I need to be getting ready."

"Getting ready for what?" asks Cameron.

"For Crocker and Ashton. They said they may be bringing some people over later."

"Oh. Well, maybe I should go. I don't want to be in the way."

Yes, maybe you should go, thinks Billy, but instead he insists that Cameron stay, assuring him that he certainly won't be in the way.

Ryan Rigsby sits in his bedroom writing new sermons and thanking God for not allowing him to be killed by the Cadillac, which had surely been piloted by one of Satan's minions.

Amanda sits at her kitchen table sipping chamomile tea. She tells herself that by the time she finishes her cup of tea, she will have decided whether or not she is going to terminate her pregnancy.

Barely a full sip remains at the bottom of her mug.

Sky and Amber sit with Ashton and Crocker. The patrons at neighboring tables buy round after round of cocktails.

Billy is drinking cocktails of his own. The newly opened bourbon bottle on the coffee table slowly disappears as Cameron, at Billy's request, talks about his years on the sailboat. The more Billy drinks, the harder it is for him not to stare. As hard as he tries to squelch the thought, he is developing an irrepressible desire to touch Cameron.

Amanda takes her last sip. She is going to have a baby.

"Let's get out of here," says Amber.

"I think I love you," says Billy, interrupting Cameron's tale of plucking six Cuban refugees out of the Atlantic, hours after their homemade raft had disintegrated in the ocean.
"What's that?" asks Cameron.
"I think I love you. That first time I saw you at the marina, there was something about you. I haven't been able to stop thinking of you since."
"You're drunk."
"That doesn't mean I don't love you."
Cameron is flabbergasted. The greatest baseball player in America has developed a crush on him, a homeless hack painter.
"I mean it," continues Billy, his eyelids drooping under the weight of the bourbon. "I'm not saying I like it, but it's true. It's what was wrong in Pittsburgh. I couldn't stop thinking about you long enough to put together a decent trip to the plate."

"So that's what was going on."

"What am I supposed to do?"

"Look, it's really not that big of a deal."

"It feels like a big deal."

"You've never been in love before, have you?"

"I think I'm in love now."

"No, you don't even know me. You've developed a bit of a crush, that's all."

"But you're all I think about."

"And we need to do something about that. I'm not going to be responsible for you blowing the greatest batting season in six decades."

"I'm just so confused," says Billy, approaching tears.

"We can fix it."

"How?"

"We'll start with the Desmondian healing ritual."

"What's that?"

"Just go to the backyard, look at the sky, and take a few deep breaths. I'll be right there."

As Billy stumbles towards the sliding glass door leading to the patio, Cameron runs upstairs and grabs two green cotton sheets from the linen closet.

"Why don't we go try to cheer up Overby," suggests Mark Crocker.

Sky is very much in favor of the idea. "Maybe Cameron will still be there, and I'll get a chance to thank him," she laughs.

Cameron comes out of the house carrying the two sheets and the bourbon bottle. "Here, take a swig," Cameron says, handing the bottle to Billy.

Billy takes the bottle and lifts it toward the clear, late-summer sky.

"Now laugh," instructs Cameron.

"What do you mean?" asks Billy.

"Just laugh."

"Laugh at what?"

"Anything. Nothing. It doesn't matter."

Billy lets out a less than impressive chortle.

"Like this," Cameron says, and he launches into a bottom-of-the-gut, full body belly laugh that fills the night sky.

Billy is sucked into Cameron's laugh, and within moments he is letting loose a hearty cackle of his own.

Ryan Rigsby shuts his Bible and prepares for sleep. "WITH YOUR STRENGTH, O GOD, I WILL WAKE TOMORROW AND LAUGH IN THE FACE OF MY ENEMIES. YOU ARE WITH ME, AND LIKE YOUR SERVANT JOB, I WILL PERSERVERE IN THE FACE OF ADVERSITY AND NEVER FORGET THAT I LIVE TO SERVE YOUR HOLY CAUSE."

"Good job," says Cameron, handing Billy one of the sheets.

"What do I do with this?" asks Billy.

"Just watch," says Cameron, pulling his shirt over his head. He steps out of his jeans and boxers, lifts his sheet above his head and begins to dance around the yard.

"He must not be home," says Gary Ashton, ringing the doorbell a second time.

"SSShhh. Listen," says Amber. "I think they're out back."

Billy removes his shirt and pants and holds his sheet above his head and watches as it rises in the breeze. "This is crazy," he calls to Cameron.

  *Full Count*

"That's the whole idea. Just let everything go."

Billy feels the frustration and confusion exit his body as he dances through his backyard. Feeling lighter than he has in years, he looks at the moon and howls with laughter.

Amber, Sky, Crocker, and Ashton follow the laughter to the iron gate leading to the backyard.

"Good Lord!" exclaims Crocker.

Amber suggests they join in, but Crocker and Ashton insist on leaving quietly.

Full Count

Suicide Squeeze

Billy wakes a bit hung over, but as images of the previous night's Desmondian healing ritual roll through his mind, he shakes his head in amused disbelief. He rises, and when he opens his bedroom door, Cameron calls from the kitchen.

"Pancakes will be up in a few minutes."

Billy pours himself a glass of juice and has a seat at the kitchen table. He thinks he should say something about the previous night, but nothing comes to mind, and Cameron doesn't mention it.

"I don't think you'll be going up against Clarence Macy again any time soon," Cameron says, breaking the silence.

"Why not?"

Cameron motions to the newspaper lying open on the table: Macy Suspected of Killing Two. "Killed his ex-fiancé and her lover in an oyster bar after a game in Atlanta last night."

Billy is stunned. "You gotta be kidding," he says, scanning the article. "He always seemed like such a nice guy."

"Last week a future murderer was firing ninety-mile-an-hour fastballs by your head. That's pretty wild."

"Yeah, it is." Billy sips his juice and imagines the crime scene, hundreds of seafood patrons, chatting away at each other about their days, and then, boom, boom, two people shot right in front of them. Billy wonders if there was much blood. Cameron flips the pancakes. The microwave dings and he removes a measuring cup half-filled with melted butter and sets it in front of Billy, who is wondering whether Diane Duncan and her lover had any idea that they wouldn't make it through the day. "You ever think about it?" asks Billy.

"About what?" asks Cameron.

"That you might die."

"All the time. But there's no 'might' to it."

"What do you mean?"

"I'm definitely going to die, and I hate to break it to you, but so are you. Absolutely no escaping it."

"What do you think it's like?"

"I don't think it's like anything. When the game's over, the game's over."

"What about Jesus and all that stuff?"

Cameron flips a pancake into the air and catches it with a plate. "Jesus knew the deal."

"So you believe in some kind of life after death?"

Cameron flips another pancake into the air and it lands on top of the first. "Not at all."

"But wasn't that Jesus' whole thing?"

"Some people think so."

"But you don't?"

Cameron sets the plate of pancakes in front of Billy and pours four fresh circles of batter on the griddle. "No, I don't."

"How do you see it, then?"

"You sure you want to get me started this early in the morning?"

"Go ahead," Billy says, trying to shake the images of Clarence Macy, children in booster seats, plates of shellfish, baskets of hush puppies, and a blood-covered hardwood floor.

"Let's say this kid looks around one day and sees that life for most people is just a frantic struggle to get a little more than what they've already got, and he decides he's going to try something different."

"Okay," Billy says, taking a bite from his stack of pancakes. "These are delicious, by the way."

  *Full Count*

"Good. So this kid gets old enough to be on his own, and he just walks away from everything: his father's trade, the village, everything. He gets out of town, the sun sets, the stars come out, and the next morning he wakes up, and he has the whole day in front of him. He's got this sense of freedom that makes his lack of a plan seem like a pretty good plan, you know what I mean? Maybe he's a little scared, a little hungry, but maybe there's enough cactus fruit or wild figs to keep him fueled."

"Sounds like a feast."

"Probably not. But he's feeling pretty smug. He's spent two decades watching the people around him, the rich, the poor, the scholars, the tradesmen; and they all look the same, kind of like they misplaced their car keys. Pardon the anachronism. And after years of dreariness, he's out in the wilderness, ecstatic to be alive. He thinks he's discovered something new."

Billy adds syrup to his pancakes. "Doesn't he get lonely?"

"Probably at times. Probably thinks about going back to town a time or two. But then he runs into another man who's been living out in the desert for years. The kid's a bit crushed that it's nothing new he's stumbled across, this escape, this freedom, but the companionship more than makes up for any disappointment, so he hangs out for a while."

"But then he gets restless again?"

Cameron flips the pancakes. "Yeah, but not before hearing a lot of good stuff from this wild desert guy who has purged himself of all the ugliness of human interaction and arrived at this place of pure love. He's been away from people long enough to lose his fear. All he has left is love, and he teaches that to the kid. The kid's smart. He gets it. The freedom's cool, but really it's about the love, and love is just the absence of fear."

"But if we all go out into the desert, then we've just moved the village somewhere else."

"You're pretty bright for a baseball player," Cameron says.

"And you're pretty smart for a homeless guy. Keep going."

"Well, the kid doesn't stay in the desert. He's got it figured out that people can be pretty decent if they get away from their fear. So, full of youthful energy, he heads back into town to change the world."

Billy pictures the waitresses in the oyster bar. Some of them have blood spattered on their white uniforms. He wonders if any of the patrons left tips as they abandoned their meals. "And it was a tougher task than he had envisioned."

"Pretty much impossible. People are pretty attached to their fear. But a few people, other young people, were willing to walk off the job and follow this guy. But they never quite got it."

Billy wonders if Macy would have killed two people if he'd been pitching better. Billy wonders if his homerun and base hits off of Macy could be in any way responsible for Diane Duncan's death. "So it was all for nothing?"

Cameron removes his pancakes from the griddle and takes a seat across from Cameron. "It was all for what it was. It was all for hope."

"Where's the hope in it?"

"The hope is that this kid left his fear in the desert. Some people hated him for it, and they tried to put his fear back in him, but he didn't let them."

"But they killed him," Billy says, wondering what Clarence Macy is thinking at the moment, wondering how Macy's teammates will be affected by the murders.

"But they didn't scare him. He loved them as he died. He pitied their fear."

 *Full Count*

"How do you know?"

"This kid figured out that the thing that really separates humans from animals is not opposable thumbs or the ability to do arithmetic, but the ability to step out from under fear. The kid overcame death by accepting it; and in exchange he got to live in that place in his mind that he found in the desert."

"So that's what it's all about, huh?"

"Maybe. Or maybe it's all about going to hell if you don't buy a house in the suburbs, raise two kids, and vote Republican."

"Hey, now, I just happen to be a registered Republican."

"Don't worry," says a smiling Cameron, "I don't imagine the kid would care which way you vote."

Cameron leaves to shower. Billy rinses the dishes and wonders who Clarence Macy shot first. Glancing out the window into the backyard, he thinks of the Desmondian healing ritual and manages to laugh a little, even though he's fully aware that his feelings for Cameron have not diminished in the slightest.

As Ryan Rigsby lambastes the sinners on Hillsborough Street, his armpits sting, rubbed raw by his crutches. His recent afflictions have bolstered his sense of righteousness, and there is unprecedented fervor in his voice:

"THEIR IDOLS ARE SILVER AND GOLD, THE WORK OF MEN'S HANDS. THEY HAVE MOUTHS BUT THEY SPEAK NOT. EYES HAVE THEY, BUT THEY SEE NOT. THEY HAVE EARS, BUT THEY HEAR NOT. NOSES HAVE THEY, BUT THEY SMELL NOT."

"I can sure smell you. You should think about bathing."

Ryan turns to see two young men, holding hands as they walk away, laughing.

"THOU SHALL NOT LIE WITH MANKIND, AS WITH WOMANKIND. IT IS ABOMINATION. LEVITICUS EIGHTEEN, TWENTY-TWO."

The young men turn and walk back toward Ryan. The taller one stands well over six feet tall. He steps close to Ryan. His nose is within six inches of Ryan's and Ryan can feel the man's breath as he speaks. "Who has also made us able ministers of the new testament; not of the letter, but of the spirit, for the letter kills, but the spirit gives life. Paul's second letter to the Corinthians. Chapter three, verse six, you self-righteous prick," the man says and then stares, not backing away.

Ryan stands silent, staring back, looking for hints of Satan behind the sodomite's squinting eyes.

When Billy leaves for the ballpark, Cameron walks to the drugstore to pick up his photos of Billy. When he returns home, he spreads the pictures on the coffee table, selects a headshot, and sets up his easel in the living room.

As Amanda stencils a large Winnie the Pooh on a wall of her former guest bedroom, she imagines a little boy bundled up for a day at the fair. The boy's wide eyes take in the rivers of people and bright lights. A large clown walks up to her son and chuckles. The boy is scared. He reaches for Amanda, and Amanda lifts him up and whispers words of comfort. Her son returns her smile and it is a perfect day. And then, through the smoked sausages, onions and peppers, through the fried dough and smoked turkey legs, a familiar scent surrounds Amanda and she turns to see Cameron approaching with a giant stuffed bear. Her son's eyes grow wider.

Amanda finishes Pooh and starts on Tigger, vowing to call Cameron by the end of the day.

"Thanks, Tim, I owe you," says Margaret to Reverend Timothy Goss, who has come in early to cover Margaret's shift. Margaret usually watches the game on the large screen in the dining room of the soup kitchen, but she's going to today's game with Cameron.

Ryan Rigsby is shambling home on his crutches, having ended his day of preaching early to allow more time for Biblical research into the sinfulness of homosexuality.

"FATHER, THOSE WHO FIGHT AGAINST YOUR GRACE ARE MANY. I PRAY YOU PROTECT ME FROM THEIR NUMBERS THAT I MAY FLOURISH IN MY EFFORTS TO SPREAD YOUR WORD," prays Ryan as he passes in front of Tony's Pawn and Gold Shop. "YOUR GLORY GIVES ME THE STRENGTH TO STAND ALONE IN THE FACE OF SATAN'S ARMY IF THAT IT IS THE ROLE YOU HAVE CHOSEN FOR ME, AND I KNOW YOU SHALL PROVIDE FOR MY SAFETY, FOR YOU ARE THE SHEPHERD OF THE SOUL OF THIS HUMBLE LAMB."

The tip of Ryan's right crutch finds a crevice in the sidewalk, interrupting his already awkward gate. Ryan falls to the ground, and as he grasps the ledge of the pawnshop window in order to pull himself up, he realizes the crevice was a part of God's plan, a part of God's answer to his prayer for protection.

On the other side of the window sits a Colt Python .357 Magnum pistol. The gun, almost a foot in length, is of the magnitude one would expect for a firearm chosen by God to do his work. If he squints a little, Ryan is fairly certain he can see a faint halo surrounding the pistol.

Mark Crocker glances inside the locker room, and seeing no one but Billy, he decides to wait outside for Gary Ashton.

Cameron is looking forward to attending the game, but he is a bit disappointed to have to leave his painting. He has become captured by the strong division of light created by Billy's brow, and by the contrast between Billy's strong features and soft eyes. He tucks the photograph into his shirt pocket and goes inside for a soda while he waits for Margaret.

Inside Tony's Pawn and Gold, Ryan attempts to negotiate a lower price for the Colt pistol.

"If I wanted to sell the gun for three hundred dollars, I would have written three hundred dollars on the price tag," says an annoyed Tony. "You want the gun, then you're going to need a license and seven hundred dollars. If that ain't good enough, you can hobble right back out the door."

"THIS GUN IS NOT FOR ME, BUT FOR THE WORK OF GOD."

"Then you tell God to bring me seven hundred dollars and a license, and the gun's his."

"I WILL RETURN FOR THE INSTRUMENT OF THE LORD," says Ryan, giving up for the time being. "YOU HAVE DELAYED ME, SATAN, BUT YOU SHALL NOT PREVAIL AGAINST THE LORD ALMIGHTY," he proclaims as he exits the pawnshop.

As Margaret and Cameron are about to leave for the game, the phone rings. It's Amanda. Cameron feels his muscles and arteries contract. He wants very much to talk to her. He also wants very much not to talk to her.

"Look, this isn't a good time. I'm on my way out," he explains.

While Cameron fields Amanda's protests, Margaret takes a peek at Cameron's partial portrait of Billy and is impressed.

"We'll talk later," says Cameron. He hangs up the phone in the middle of Amanda's objection, and he and Margaret leave for the ballpark.

When Billy comes to the plate in the bottom of the first against Chicago southpaw Tracy Arrington, he feels like his old self. He plants his right foot in the back of the box, and as he gives it the ritualistic three twists, he uses thoughts of the Desmondian healing ritual to chase away thoughts of the Macy murders. He shoulders his bat, and as his left foot moves into the box, his mind is clear except for the small part that is noticing that it's been a while since he has had such a clear mind.

Arrington's first pitch fastball seems to travel towards the plate in slow motion, and Billy's hips, forearms, and wrists orchestrate a fluid swing that greets the ball solidly and sends it into the right field gap for a two-out double, scoring Dale Currin from first.

Cameron enjoys watching the game with Margaret. He enjoys her conversation between innings and appreciates her focused silence during play.

"I'm glad you're staying with Billy for a while," she says after Waves first baseman Ron Brown flies out to end the fourth inning.

"Why's that?" asks Cameron, signaling to the hot dog vendor for two hot dogs.

"You seem like an interesting person. You seem like a gentle person. I just think it's good for Billy to be around people who think about more than baseball, women, and booze."

The hotdogs make their way, fan by fan, from the vendor to Cameron, who hands one hot dog to Margaret and gives the red-headed woman beside him a five dollar bill to pass back toward the vendor. " So you've met Mark Crocker."

Margaret laughs. "Now, I've got nothing against Mark. I think he's a pretty good-natured fellow, but maybe a bit limited, that's all. I just think it's good for Billy to be around people who have a perspective that extends beyond some silly game."

"I'm flattered, but if you call baseball a silly game again, I may have to go sit somewhere else."

Margaret laughs, and she and Cameron enjoy their hot dogs in silence as the fifth inning begins.

Amanda has used the anger of having been hung up on by Cameron to good use. She has completed not only the stenciling, but she has finished painting the walls, as well. To celebrate she pours herself a gin and tonic with lots of lime juice and smells it for several minutes before dumping it down the sink.

Ryan Rigsby sits down with his mother and father and says grace before dinner:

"O FATHER, THANK YOU FOR THE MEAL BEFORE US, AND THANK YOU FOR ALL OF YOUR MANY BLESSINGS, AND KEEP US MINDFUL THAT WHILE YOU GIVE ENDLESSLY OF YOUR BOUNTY OF GRACE, SOMETIMES WE MUST GIVE IN RETURN. TO LIVE, AS YOU WOULD HAVE US LIVE, SOMETIMES DEMANDS SACRIFICES, AND SOMETIMES THOSE SACRIFICES ARE MONETARY. AMEN."

As Ryan passes the mashed potatoes to his father, he asks for a seven hundred dollar loan.

Billy bats five for six as the Waves route Chicago by a score of nine to one, and reporters keep him in the post-game press conference for almost an hour. Afterwards, Crocker and Ashton are nowhere to be found.

Having had his loan request rejected by his father, Ryan Rigsby balances his checkbook and is disappointed when the arithmetic reveals a seventy-five dollar balance in his checking account.

After a short prayer for guidance, Ryan pulls a credit card application from his wastebasket. After completing the application, he pens a letter to Born Again Living Ministries and asks if they might return the donations he has sent them over the past year. He assures them that he needs the refund for a holy cause.

Amanda tries to reach Cameron.

The phone rings, but Cameron does not stop painting. Listening to Margaret Overby talk about her son has made Cameron feel more familiar with his subject, and by the time Billy gets home, the portrait has started to come alive.

"Can I take a look?" Billy asks, pouring himself a drink.

"Not yet."

"When?"

"It should be ready in a couple of days, maybe by tomorrow. Great game tonight."

"Thanks. I felt good out there. I think I've got my swing back. How was Mom?"

"We had a good time. She said she's glad I'm here."

"So am I."

"Then so am I."

As Billy sips his cocktail, Cameron studies his face and adds some touches to the portrait.

"I can't stop thinking about Clarence Macy murdering those two people for no reason," says Billy, despite the fact that Cameron has asked him to hold still.

"What do you mean by 'no reason'?"

"Well, I know he and his fiancée had been together for a while, but, how can you kill someone just because they start seeing someone else?"

"Macy's a chimp?"

"Whadda you mean he's a chimp."

"Some of us are bonobos. Some of us are chimps."

"What's a bonobo?"

"Bonobos and chimps are close cousins. They're both ninety-eight percent similar to us, from a DNA perspective, but chimps are a very violent species. Murder and even infanticide are pretty common among chimps, but the bonobos rarely resort to physical violence."

"Which are you?"

"I prefer to be a bonobo, but I think you've got to be ready to be a chimp around other chimps."

"Where'd you learn so much?"

"I guess when you live on a boat for years by yourself, you spend a lot of time reading and thinking about relatively useless stuff."

"I don't think it's useless. I think it's interesting."

"Just because it's interesting doesn't mean it's not useless," Cameron says, draping a sheet gently over the portrait.

"Finished?"

"Almost," says Cameron, going to the kitchen to pour himself a drink.

With Cameron in the other room, Billy finds the courage to bring up the previous night's activities. "I hope I didn't make you uncomfortable last night."

"Did I seem uncomfortable?" Cameron calls from the kitchen.

Billy laughs. "No, I guess I'm the one who feels uncomfortable."

"Look, I saved your life. At least in your mind I did. So now you have all of these feelings of gratitude and you

don't know what to do with them. But, listen, I'm the one who should be feeling all the gratitude. Things would have been pretty tough for me right now if you hadn't taken me in."

"What about your parents? You could have stayed with them for a while, couldn't you?"

"I told you, we don't get along."

"But they wouldn't have turned you away."

Cameron comes back into the room and leans back in the recliner, spilling a few drops of his gin and tonic on his chest. "The last thing my parents said to me was that they never wanted to see me again."

"You're kidding."

"Doesn't make for a very funny joke."

"Why did they say it?"

"My father found out I was involved with another man. He told my mother she could stay in contact with me if she wanted, but that if she did, he was through with her. She chose him."

"You're kidding."

"Again, it doesn't make for a very funny joke."

"That's awful."

"It's just the way things are. Look, you know why the bonobos get along so well?"

"Why?"

"Two reasons. First, the women are in charge. No one's quite sure why. The males are bigger and have two huge canines that the females don't have. So it's not a matter of physical dominance."

"So, you think the world would be a better place if women ran everything?"

"Who knows, but it works for the bonobos."

"What's the second reason?"

"Bonobos work their aggression out through sex. Two

bonobos have a conflict, they talk it over, and then they spend a few minutes bumping genitals."

"Really?"

"It's more affectionate than erotic, but it's still the kind of thing that would freak out a chimp. My father's a chimp. He can't help it."

"Who's smarter?"

"You mean me or my father?"

Billy laughs. "No, between the chimps and bonobos."

"Actually, it depends. The bonobos seem to be more gifted in communication and social skills, but the chimps seem to be better at mazes and tool use, that sort of thing."

"So the apes making the bombs have a hard time speaking to one another."

"Not a very comforting thought, is it? There are a lot of chimps in the world."

"I'll remember that."

"You should."

Cameron and Billy have another cocktail and move the subject of their conversation away from primate politics. But even as they recount the Waves' victory over Chicago, Billy has flashes of bonobo-like fantasies.

That night in his dreams, Ryan has fantasies of firing a cannon into a crowd of sinners.

That night in her dreams, Amanda has fantasies about raising a child with a yellow bear that smells like Cameron.

On Sunday morning, Margaret Overby rises, takes her daily four-mile walk, eats breakfast, and goes to church. Reverend Timothy's sermon is on tolerance.

After church, Margaret goes to the soup kitchen. She had hoped to go to the ballpark again with Cameron, but

Reverend Timothy is officiating an afternoon wedding and can't cover her shift.

Billy is backing down the drive in his Acura NSX, and decides to try one more time to convince Cameron, who is mowing the grass, to ride in with him to see the doubleheader.

"Why don't you cut the grass tomorrow?" Billy calls out.

Cameron turns off the mower. "What?"

"Why don't you cut the grass tomorrow? Tomorrow's an off day."

"Some of us don't have off days," replies Cameron, knowing that it's a silly statement coming from someone who's unemployed. His real reason for staying home is his desire to finish Billy's portrait. Cameron wishes Billy good luck and heads back to the mower.

Ryan Rigsby stands in his regular Sunday morning corner of Pullen Park, preaching to the sky. There have been brief intervals in Ryan's ministry when he actually accumulated a regular or two who would appear on successive Sundays to hear his message, but that was in a less sinful world.

Cameron sits down to chat with Gary Ashton before the first game of the doubleheader, but after an exchange of hellos, Ashton excuses himself to get his ankle taped.

Amanda takes a deep breath and dials Billy Overby's number.

Cameron mows away in the backyard as the phones ring inside.

Amanda slams the phone down and pops in her yoga tape.

Over the course of the next several hours, Billy gets at least one hit off of seven different Chicago pitchers. He finishes the doubleheader nine for twelve with eight runs batted in.

As Cameron watches Billy on television explaining to reporters that his recent turnaround at the plate is in some part due to the realization that fear is something one can learn to let go of, he studies the outline of Billy's nose and strokes on the final touches of the portrait.

Ryan Rigsby kneels on his bedroom floor praying for strength.
"DEAR GOD, I CHERISH THE CHALLENGES YOU PROVIDE TO BUILD MY STRENGTH IN THE SPIRIT, BUT I PRAY, SHOULD YOU FIND IT USEFUL IN YOUR PLANS, THAT THE VILEST OF FATES BEFALL THE SKATEBOARDING SON OF SATAN WHO FIRST LURED ME INTO THE STREET TO BE STRUCK DOWN BY ONE OF HIS SATANIC BRETHREN, AND NOW HAS SEEN FIT TO MAKE OFF WITH ONE OF MY CRUTCHES. AND FATHER, I PRAY THAT YOU WILL PROVIDE THE MONETARY MANNA WHICH WILL ENABLE ME TO PURCHASE THE HOLY FIREARM TO WHICH YOU HAVE DIRECTED ME. AMEN."

Billy is astounded by the portrait. Plenty of people have sought his photograph, and a few have even done paintings of him, but they have always been done with the commercial gain of the photographer, painter, or Waves franchise in mind.

"If you don't like it, I thought you could give it to your mother."

"I love it."

"Good. I wasn't sure what you'd think about it. I'm glad you like it."

"Like it. It's incredible. How did you do it?" asks Billy, unable to fathom how tubes of oil paint could be transformed into something so lifelike, into something that seems to capture the spirit of something he feels inside himself.

Cameron is pleased with Billy's reaction. "I don't know. I just look at the light and put down what I see."

"This is the greatest present anyone has ever given me."

"Well, I really appreciate you let—" begins Cameron as Billy gives him an appreciative hug.

But as Billy embraces Cameron, a trigger flips somewhere in Billy's mind. As he breathes in Cameron's scent, as he thinks about the time and effort that went into the painting, his brain is filled with something beyond thought. Cameron's heroics aboard *Screwball III*, Diane Duncan losing her life in an oyster bar, and the Desmondian healing ritual are but a small part of the montage that permeates Billy's mind. As his thoughts turn to a buzz of excitement, Billy finds Cameron's lips with his.

Cameron's first instinct is to repel the kiss, but in the briefest of moments, Billy's passion is transferred through his lips to Cameron, and Cameron knows that there is something undeniable, something holy, in such a kiss, and he gives in.

Full Count

Bottom of the Ninth

Billy wakes early. He feels more than a little frightened. But happy. Very, very happy.

After several minutes he decides to wake Cameron. "Cameron, wake up, I've got an idea," he says, nudging Cameron's shoulder.

Cameron rolls over. "What is it?"

"Let's go to the beach."

Cameron sits up. He misses the ocean. "That sounds like a great idea, but aren't you flying out tonight?"

"We don't have to be at the airport until ten."

"What are we waiting for then?"

Ryan Rigsby is jolted by the headline on the front page of the sports section which drapes Paul Rigsby as he reads the box scores. *Overby Approaches 400.*

Ryan had thought that Overby's slump was a sign that there was still time for humankind to change its ways, but Ryan sees that he was perhaps being overly optimistic. God is stepping in so that the unbreakable may be broken, and the end of the world might be only a couple of dozen ballgames away.

As soon as his father leaves for work, Ryan asks his mother to take him to the sheriff's office.

"Are you in trouble, son?"

"THE SIGNS ARE EVERYWHERE. THE END IS NEAR, MOTHER. WE ARE ALL IN TROUBLE."

Cameron merges Billy's Acura NSX onto I-40.

"So, where we headed?" asks Billy.

"East," says Cameron, pressing the accelerator closer to the floor.

Amanda tries to call Cameron, but once again there is no answer at Billy Overby's number. Amanda wonders if Cameron is even in Raleigh.

At the sheriff's office, Ryan completes his pistol permit and returns it to the deputy at the counter.

"Thank you, Mr. Rigsby," says the deputy. "We'll call you when the permit is finalized."

"I SHALL WAIT," says Ryan. "THE LORD SMILES UPON THE PATIENT."

"There's a seven day processing and waiting period, Mr. Overby. We'll call you when your permit is finalized."

"DAMN YOU, SATAN!" Ryan exclaims to the walls.

As Ryan leaves, the deputy makes a note at the top of Ryan's application: Check for history of involuntary commitment.

At the soup kitchen, Margaret sits over a lunch of baked chicken quarters, rice, and fruit salad with Reverend Timothy and his friend, Rabbi Joseph Greene.

"You know, Margaret, there's only one problem with Christians," the rabbi says good-naturedly.

"What's that?" Margaret asks.

"Christians take their religion too seriously," says the rabbi.

Reverend Timothy laughs. Margaret asks Reverend Timothy what he thinks of the rabbi's assertion.

"He may have a point."

"Of course, I have a point, my friend. You cannot deny that your folks sometimes have difficulty distinguishing between myth and history, and your bible is certainly filled with both."

"I don't think it's solely a Christian phenomena. And if a myth works better as a fact, who am I to disagree?"

"You are a spiritual leader, my friend, that's who."

"And a fine one at that," says Margaret, smiling as she places a hand on Reverend Timothy's shoulder.

"And what do you do when someone in your temple asks whether Eden is myth or historical fact?" inquires Reverend Timothy.

"Oh, my friend, that's just it," laughs Rabbi Greene. "In forty-seven years, I've never been asked."

Ryan Rigsby has his mother drive him to K-Mart.

"You wait here. I'll be right back," he says, shutting the door of the station wagon.

Inside, Ryan goes to the sporting goods counter and asks for a box of .357 caliber bullets.

Having driven at an average speed of ninety miles an hour, Cameron and Billy make it to Emerald Isle in under two hours. Cameron pulls into a fishing pier parking lot, and he and Billy grab their towels and small cooler and head for the beach. They walk several hundred yards to find a spot away from the sprinkling of Monday morning beach goers near the pier. Before sitting down, Billy pulls a bottle from the cooler, fills a plastic cup with ice and pink liquid, and hands the cup to Cameron.

"What is this, anyway?" asks Cameron.

"Gin and pink lemonade," Billy says, filling a cup for himself.

"Sounds like one of Crocker's recipes."

"My mother's actually. She says it was one of my father's favorite things about summer."

Cameron takes a sip. "Not bad. They should serve this at the soup kitchen."

"I'm sure it would be a favorite," says Billy, taking a long sip before leaning back and enjoying the contrast of the sun's rays and the coolness of the cup resting on his chest.

Ryan, leaning on his single crutch, stands in front of the pawnshop, having decided to preach within sight of what he has come to think of as his pistol. "MOREOVER, THE WORD OF THE LORD CAME UNTO ME, SAYING, WHAT SEEST THOU? AND I SAID, I SEE A SEETHING POT, AND THE LORD SAID UNTO ME, THOU HAST WELL SEEN," exclaims Ryan, jangling the bullets in his pocket. "AND THE LORD HAS SAID UNTO ME, I SHALL SEND YE A SNAKE WITH WHICH YOU SHALL DESTROY THE SERPENT." Ryan salivates a little as he steals a glimpse of the Colt Python .357 Magnum.

Billy Overby, drunk on gin and life, hurdles a series of breakers as he sprints into the Atlantic Ocean. As he splashes in the surf, he feels happier—or at least happy in a different way—than he has ever felt before. He looks back to the beach and motions to Cameron to join him. Cameron waves and takes a sip of his gin.

Billy leans back and lets himself bob on the incoming swells. He smiles as the weight of himself disappears.

Amanda leans back, surrounded by the scent of lavender. As she soaks, she tries to let go of everything except the life growing inside her. She tells herself that it will be better for everyone—her, the baby, and Cameron—if she never even tells Cameron that he's going to be a father. She tells herself this again. And again. She has almost convinced herself that it is true when she rises from the tub to go to the phone.

No answer.

She sits and cries, lavender bubbles slowly sliding down her back.

Billy enjoys the near burn of the hot sand as he walks back toward Cameron.

After several minutes of standing above Cameron, watching his chest rise and fall, Billy extends his arm and points a finger down at Cameron's belly, allowing a drop of ocean to fall and jolt Cameron awake.

Ryan stiffens as he sees the gay couple from the previous day walking toward him. He looks toward the Python Magnum to find strength. In a week it will be mine, he thinks. He prays for strength as he takes a deep breath. "THERE SHALL BE NO WHORE OF THE DAUGHTERS OF ISRAEL, NOR A SODOMITE OF THE SONS OF ISRAEL."

The two men appear to be ignoring him when the tall one spits. Ryan is appalled to have the saliva of a sodomite dripping from his nose. He raises his crutch, but before he can take a swing, the smaller man punches Ryan in the gut, dropping him to his knees.

"WITHIN THE COURSE OF SEVEN DAYS, VENGANCE SHALL BE MINE," he calls as the couple walks away.

"You just don't get it, do you?" says Cameron, moving away from Billy.

"What exactly is it that I don't get?"

"Everything. Your whole damn life. There is no room for me in your life, can't you understand that?"

"Maybe you mean there's no room for me in your life."

"This is absolutely incredible. Look, if you were selling insurance or running a body shop or managing a restaurant, we just might have something very nice. But you're Billy Overby. You are the batting leader of major league baseball, which, whether you like it or not, makes you the poster boy of every testosterone-stuffed he-man in the nation, which, again, whether you like it or not, means you can't go around kissing boys."

Billy sits up. "You're scared."

"Absolutely. I'm scared for you."

"That's not fair. I'm not scared."

"But you should be. What, you think this is some game. You think you can be some goddam queer Jackie Robinson? Well, guess what, even if that were possible, who says I want to play along? And, anyway, it's not possible. A little pigment is nothing compared to a nation of angry men turning on the television to see that the man they've dreamed of being for months has a thing for other men."

"Jesus Christ, Cameron, this is the twenty-first century."

"It could be three thousand and three, but Mark Crocker would still be a Neanderthal. Evolution hasn't gone cyber. What do you think would happen if you went into the locker room tomorrow and told the team you're dating a man?"

"I don't know."

"Then you're a fool," says Cameron, rising and walking down the beach.

Ryan Rigsby hobbles up and down Hillsborough Street, preaching the word, fueled by an even greater certainty that the end is near.

The further Cameron walks, the guiltier he feels. The one thing he has always believed in is love. He believed in it enough to think he and Amanda could spend a lifetime

together despite their differences. He believes in it enough to think that his parents might call one day, full of remorse. He believes in it enough to think that life, even in a world filled with chaos and violence, is a wonderful thing. Yet he told Billy his love was no good, misguided.

When Cameron arrives back at their towels, Billy has finished the rest of the gin and pink lemonade. Cameron starts to apologize, but Billy interrupts.

"I've got a plan," says Billy.

"And what's that?"

"Just give me a few minutes. Just go swimming with me. Don't be scared, for me or you, until we get out of the water."

"That sounds reasonable," Cameron says.

A young girl walks her Irish setter near the waterline. After she passes, Cameron and Billy dash for the water.

At the soup kitchen, Reverend Timothy rinses dishes and runs them through the commercial sanitizer while Margaret removes clean dishes and puts them on the shelves.

"Margaret, what do you think the congregation would think if I officiated a wedding for a gay couple?" asks Reverend Timothy as he scrapes a stubborn piece of food from a plate.

"Now that's a good question. Is this hypothetical, or has a couple approached you?"

"My nephew. He hasn't actually asked, but I can tell he'd like me to volunteer."

"Tim, I can't imagine most people would care one way or the other."

"But some would."

Margaret puts down a stack of saucers. "The way I see it, thousands of people in this country have died at the hands of terrorists. The murder rate is rising. In general, the world is in no short supply of hate. So if someone has a problem with anybody proclaiming their love for anybody else, I can't see that losing them would be any great blow to the church."

"That's hard to argue with."

"But some people will try. I'll feel it out and let you know what I hear."

"You're a good friend," says Reverend Timothy.

"Not that much better than you deserve," Margaret says with a smile.

The saltwater nourishes Cameron. He lets a large wave carry him towards shore and then swims back out and jumps into Billy's arms. Billy catches Cameron and presses him towards the sky, then lowers him into a frantic embrace. Their arms pull hard, as if trying to draw the other's body into their own. They rise and fall with the incoming swells.

Margaret and Reverend Timmy lock the doors of the soup kitchen, Amanda tries once again to call Cameron, and Ryan preaches relentlessly to Hillsborough Street's unfaithful.

Having fallen asleep after their swim and awakened to a sky painted orange and red by a setting sun, Cameron and Billy race towards Raleigh at over a hundred miles an hour to insure that Billy will not miss the team's flight to Colorado. They arrive at the airport only minutes before the scheduled departure.

On the plane, Billy's drunkenness and infatuation keep him from making much out of the fact that Ashton and Crocker do not occupy the usual seats nearby.

Cameron sits staring at the portrait of Billy and reflecting on the fact that the thin membrane that had contained his feelings for Billy has been punctured. He is beautiful, funny, and intelligent, thinks Cameron. If only he weren't about to become one of the most famous baseball players in history.

Bases Loaded

Ryan Rigsby wakes full of fear. He prays for the strength to get out of bed, but the thought of facing another day's worth of sinners, particularly violent sodomites, fills him with a paralyzing dread.

Cameron wakes calm and relaxed. As he allows the remnants of sleep to drift away, he thinks of how refreshing the ocean had been, and how absolutely outlandish is the nature of life.

Cameron's sense of well being follows him to the kitchen, where he fries two eggs and several strips of bacon.

His sense of well being follows him to the patio, where he stretches lazily in the morning sun.

His sense of well being follows him down the drive to get the newspaper, but when he sees the photograph on the front page, that sense of well being is shattered.

Having finally forced himself out of bed, Ryan takes a seat at the breakfast table across from his newspaper-shrouded father. Ryan is about to swallow his first spoonful of cornflakes when he notices the photograph on the front page.

He chokes.

Cameron reads the caption: Batting leader Billy Overby spends off day rejuvenating at coast with friend.

Cameron translates: You tell us; is Billy Overby gay, or what?

Ryan studies the photograph of Billy Overby holding his "friend" towards the sky as a wave prepares to break over them.

Ryan is not exactly sure about all of the details of God's plan for him, but he is certain of three things: It has something to do with Billy Overby, sodomites, and the Colt Python.

Amanda has been studying the front page for about half an hour. Her evaluation of Billy's expression is clear: He's in love with Cameron.

But it's Cameron's face that she can't quite decipher. As she stares at the picture, Cameron's expression seems to vacillate between infatuation and confusion. She tells herself that she is the source of the confusion.

Cameron calls the phone number Billy left.

"You know, it's not even six in the morning here," Billy says, his voice hoarse with sleep.

"Well, I'm afraid you might as well get ready for a good bit of unpleasantness today." Cameron tells Billy about the picture. "Listen to me. I'm crazy. I saved your life, and you felt obligated to help me out for a while. You had no idea I was crazy, and you had no idea I was attracted to you until I started jumping on you in the water. You're obviously attempting to fend me off in the photograph. As soon as we got back to Raleigh, you told me I had to be out by noon today. You got it?"

There are several seconds of silence on the line.

At Tony's Pawn and Gold, Ryan explains to Tony that things have grown more urgent. Tony explains that he doesn't give a damn.

Reverend Timothy knocks on Margaret's door.

"Hello, Timothy."

"I just wanted to come by and make sure you were doing all right."

"Is there some reason I shouldn't be?"

Reverend Timothy holds out the morning paper. Margaret looks at it and sits down, worried about the trouble that is undoubtedly headed Billy's way.

"Billy, I just talked to Coach Simmons. He says there's a picture of you and some man on the front page of today's paper. What in the hell's going on? Is it Cameron?"

Billy begins to tell Crocker about how he'd just found out that Cameron was gay and how he told him not to be there when he gets back.

Crocker interrupts. "Look, Billy, we've been friends a long time. At least I thought we were friends. But damn, Billy, I saw you dancing in your backyard the other night, and it made me sick."

"I don't know what you're talking about."

"Ashton was there, too. And Sky and Amber. Look, I'm sorry Billy, you can do whatever you got to do, but I just can't be your friend any more. What would people think? I can't be hanging around a damn fairy. I just can't."

"I'm telling you, I—"

"I told Coach I'd talk to you, and now I have. I gotta go." Crocker, who has not looked at Billy since entering the room, turns and leaves.

The doorbell rings. Cameron looks out the window and sees several reporters in the front yard. He throws as many of his belongings as he can in his backpack and leaves through the back door.

On the bus ride to the stadium, no one speaks to Billy. He feels a wave of whispers and laughter build from the back of the bus and tumble towards him.

Cameron walks. He has no idea where he's going and does not care.

Waves owner Nick Densby has flown to Colorado and is waiting for Billy at the stadium. They step into an empty office off of the locker room.

"Christ, Billy. This is money. I don't give a damn about what floats your boat. For the most part it's none of my business, but we got a good thing going here. We can win the pennant and you can go down in the record books as the best damn player in the last sixty years. Listen, Billy, you know what that could mean to this organization? I'm not here to judge you, son, but I am telling you this: I don't care if you bat a goddamned thousand, we aren't renewing your contract if you're more interested in your goddam love life than you are in what's best for this team, hell, not just for the team, but for all of baseball, and I wouldn't count on any other franchise opening their arms for the game's first openly gay player. I think you get my point."

"Your point is very clear."

"I'm glad, Billy."

Cameron takes a break from his day of walking to watch the game in a department store. The Waves go down in order in the top of the first. Colorado scores one in the bottom of the inning.

As the second inning begins, Cameron stands in the middle of the television display, surrounded by dozens of images of Billy stepping to the plate.

As Billy steps to the plate, shouts of "faggot" sift

through the crowd noise. Steve Gagnon, who was called up from the Colorado triple-A team to replace Macy, fires a fastball across the middle of the plate for strike one.

Billy steps out of the box and thinks about everything except the next pitch. He thinks about how a double homicide was a boon for Gagnon's career. He thinks about how he learned to play baseball from a man he can't remember. He thinks about how the same people who can worship him for hitting a piece of rawhide into an area of a field unmanned by the opposing team can hate him for touching another human of his own gender. These thoughts are not overwhelming, but liberating. Billy laughs.

For the next two days, Cameron walks, ducking from anyone who seems to recognize him as the man in the ocean with Billy Overby.

For the next two days, Ryan preaches, fueled by the thought that his gun permit and his new credit card should arrive soon.

For the next two days, Amanda tries to call Cameron at Billy Overby's and gets no answer.

For the next two days, Billy slanders a man he loves and tallies six hits as his appreciation for the absurd continues to grow and his batting average rises to within five points of four hundred.

Cameron develops a routine of walking throughout the night and sleeping in parks during the day. He has thirty-seven dollars left in his pocket when he passes the Billy Overby Foundation Soup Kitchen. Margaret Overby's car is parked outside.

Cameron decides not to go in.

Inside the soup kitchen, Margaret Overby watches the large-screen television and is relieved to see that the press is beginning to return its focus to Billy's batting average, rather than speculations about his love life. Margaret wonders where Cameron is and prays that he's all right.

Billy returns to an empty house. He spends the evening drinking gin and pink lemonade.

As Cameron walks down Hillsborough Street, he can see in some of the classroom buildings across the street. He is struck by the variations of student expressions from one classroom to the next. He thinks about how he would consider signing up for a literature class if he weren't homeless with only thirty-seven dollars in his pocket.

"I KNOW THY WORKS AND THY LABOUR, AND THY PATIENCE, AND HOW THOU CANST NOT BEAR THEM WHICH ARE EVIL; AND THOU HAST TRIED THEM WHICH SAY THEY ARE APOSTLES, AND ARE NOT, AND HAST FOUND THEM LIARS." Ryan pauses as Tony walks out of the pawnshop and locks the door. "WITHIN THE WEEK I SHALL BRING GOLD FOR THAT WHICH THE LORD DEEMS MINE."

Tony is pretending not to be aware that Ryan is speaking to him when he jumps out of the way of a skateboarder on the sidewalk. Tony also pretends not to see the skateboarder grab Ryan's remaining crutch and strike him over the head with it.

The doorbell rings. Billy opens the door to find Sky and Amber.

"We thought a little female company might be good for your public relations," says Amber.

Billy, appreciative of the gesture, asks them to come in. "But the public can go screw themselves as far as I'm concerned."

Cameron comes across a man stretched out on a park bench, whimpering. The man has a cast on his leg and appears to be bleeding from the temple. He taps the man on the shoulder. "Are you all right?"

At first, Ryan is speechless, but then everything becomes clear. God has waited for this, Ryan's loneliest hour, to set His divine plan into action. "YOU STAND BEFORE ME, SATAN, AND I AM NOT AFRAID."

Cameron, though confused by the outburst, is glad to see the man so responsive. "I was just making sure you were all right."

"YOU SHALL NOT DECEIVE ME, SODOMITE."

Cameron begins to walk off.

Ryan feels God's spirit move him. He ignores the searing pain in his femur as he hobbles to a parked motorcycle and grabs the helmet from the handlebars. The pain grows as he charges toward the window of the pawnshop, but Ryan is filled with ecstasy as he smashes the window with the helmet.

"HE HATH ALSO PREPARED FOR HIM THE INSTRUMENTS OF DEATH: HE ORDAINETH HIS ARROWS AGAINST THE PERSECUTORS. PSALM SEVEN, THIRTEEN," shouts Ryan as he uses the helmet to smash into the gun case.

Cameron stands in shock as the stranger pulls a large pistol from the hole in the window.

Ryan reaches into his pocket and retrieves a handful of bullets, some of which drop to the ground as he shoves others into the chambers of his God-given revolver. When the gun is loaded, he points the gun at Cameron. "TAKE ME TO HE WHO SEEKS TO BREAK THE UNBREAKABLE."

At the soup kitchen, Margaret fills a casserole dish with roast beef, candied carrots, and potato salad to take to Billy after she closes.

At Billy's, Sky and Amber have finished their second gin and lemonade and are trying to convince Billy to teach them the Desmondian healing ritual, but Billy's just not in the mood.

Cameron and Ryan ride the city bus towards North Raleigh. As Ryan inhales what he is certain is the scent of the devil, he presses the barrel of his Python further into Cameron's rib cage.

Lee Edwards, a rookie photographer for the *News and Observer*, parks his Ford Taurus on the side of the street in front of Billy's house.

Ryan and Cameron exit the city bus about a half-mile from Billy's house. As Ryan drapes an arm around Cameron's neck for support, a woman jogs by on the other side of the street, long legs extending from jogging shorts which cling to her athletic legs, her bare midriff rippling below a knotted tee-shirt.
"GOD HAS GIVEN YOU A TEMPLE AND YOU ALLOW SATAN TO USE IT AS A FACTORY FOR LUST. CHANGE YOUR WAYS, SISTER. CHANGE THEM NOW WHILE THERE IS STILL TIME."

"Thanks for the compliment," the woman shouts back without breaking her stride.

Sky goes out to the car for cigarettes. When she returns, she reports the Ford Taurus parked out front.

Amber smiles. "Come with me," she says to Billy, taking his hand and leading him to the couch along one of the large front windows. She tells Billy to lie down, then straddles him as she slowly removes her blouse.

Lee Edwards focuses his telephoto lens and snaps away. He is so entranced by the erotic silhouette that he doesn't notice the pair of men who hobble by him and down the drive like the losers of a drunken three-legged race.

"Hey, it's Cameron!" Sky exclaims as she opens the door. Amber and Billy spring from the couch, but their excitement is curbed when Ryan Rigsby waves his gun.

"WHEREFORE GOD ALSO GAVE THEM UP TO UNCLEANNESS THROUGH THE LUSTS OF THEIR OWN HEARTS, TO DISHONOUR THEIR OWN BODIES BETWEEN THEMSELVES, ROMANS ONE, VERSE TWENTY-FOUR," recites Ryan, unable to take his eyes off of Amber as she hooks her bra and buttons her blouse.

Amanda, out of habit more than hope, dials Billy Overby's number.

Ryan points the Python at Billy and directs him to answer the phone. "PRONOUNCE THE INITIATION OF GOD'S PLAN."

"Yes, he's here," Billy says, "but this isn't a good time."

Amanda slams down the phone and heads for her car. God's plan or not—whatever that meant—she's going to talk to Cameron.

Reverend Tim finishes mopping the kitchen and helps Margaret finish sweeping the dining area. As they lock up, he takes Margaret's hand. "Tell Billy I'm thinking about him. Tell him I'm proud of him."

Margaret kisses his cheek. "Thanks, Tim."

The doorbell rings.

Ryan directs everyone to the kitchen and orders Billy to answer the door.

"I need to speak to Cameron," says Amanda.

"This isn't a good time," Billy says, trying to hide his nervousness.

"I'm sure it isn't, but I still need to speak to him."

"Really, this isn't a good time."

"Look, there isn't going to be a good time to tell him what I need to tell him."

"Why don't you call in a few hours?" Billy says, shutting the door in Amanda's face.

Amanda is furious. Billy Overby seemed a little excited, maybe a little out of breath. "I bet it's not a good time," she says to herself, her anger growing as she stomps towards her car.

"HERE I STAND, AN OBEDIENT SERVANT OF THE LORD, AMID THIS FORSAKEN HERD OF FORNICATORS. MAY GOD'S WILL—" Ryan rolls his eyes when the doorbell rings again. He waves the Python in warning and sends Billy back to the door.

"I think you know I'll use this if I have to," Amanda says, pumping a shell into the barrel of her shotgun. "Now, let me speak to Cameron."

Billy backs into the house and Amanda follows.

Ryan points the Python at Amanda. "PRESERVE MY

LIFE FROM FEAR OF THE ENEMY. PSALM SIXTY-FOUR."

"What's going on?" Amanda demands.

"He told you this wasn't a good time," Cameron says.

"DROP YOUR WEAPON, AGENT OF SATAN. YOU CANNOT SAVE THESE SODOMITES FROM THE GRASP OF GOD."

As Lee Edwards calls his editor and tells him to call the police and send a reporter, another car arrives and parks behind the car belonging to the woman who just walked into the house with a shotgun.

Margaret Overby rings the bell before stepping through the open door with her casserole dish. "Goodness, what do we have here?" she asks as she surveys the situation.

A stranger, with a cast on his leg and streaks of dried blood on his cheek, holds a gun to Cameron's head. A woman, about whom Margaret thinks she detects the glow of pregnancy, points a shotgun at Cameron and the stranger. Billy and two young women are lying on the floor.

"BE YOU OF SATAN OR THE LORD?" asks the stranger.

"Cameron, Billy, what's going on?" asks Margaret.

"WOMAN OF SATAN. LIE DOWN WITH YOUR EVIL BRETHREN."

"The first thing I'm going to do, young man, is put this food in the refrigerator."

Ryan trains the gun on Margaret as she walks through the living area to the kitchen. "Now someone tell me what's going on," she says when she returns.

"SILENCE, WOMAN, CONSUMER OF SATAN'S APPLE."

"That's enough," says Billy, rising slowly from the floor. "I don't know exactly what you want, but there's no reason to speak that way to my mother."

"What exactly do you want?" asks Amber from the floor.

"I AM HERE TO PERFORM GOD'S WILL."

"And what would that be?" asks Amanda.

"SILENCE," says Ryan, pointing the large barrel of the Python at Amanda.

"Now, young man, I have a hard time believing that it's God's will to go pointing that gun of yours at a woman who is with child."

"With child?" asks Cameron. Ryan's arm tightens around his neck, but Cameron continues with what air he can muster. "Is that true?"

"How did you know?" Amanda asks Margaret.

"SILENCE, SINNERS." Ryan fires a shot through the ceiling for emphasis.

Lee Edwards, who is making his way along the side of the house, drops to the ground when he hears the shot.

After a few minutes of silence, he continues to the back of the house, hoping to get a view, and maybe some Pulitzer-prize pictures, of whatever's going on inside.

A stream of whispered prayer moves along Ryan's lips as the others watch silently.

The praying stops.

"AND YE SHALL HAVE A SACRIFICE MADE BY FIRE," announces Ryan, cocking the hammer of the Python and placing it firmly against Cameron's temple. "HE WHO REEKS OF SATAN'S SCENT MUST DIE TO SAVE YE WHICH HE HAS INFECTED."

The same instinct that allows Billy to anticipate fastballs and curves, is now telling him that Ryan is serious about shooting Cameron. "I'm the one you want," Billy says, taking a step towards Ryan. "I am the one you must take."

Ryan swings the gun toward Billy.

"No, I am the one," says Margaret, in an attempt to draw the gun away from her son.

But Billy takes another step toward Ryan.

"STOP, OR YOU SHALL FEEL THE WRATH OF GOD'S HOLY FIRE."

Billy knows Ryan is serious, but he puts his fear aside and takes another step closer. And another.

"I WARNED—" starts Ryan, as Billy leaps toward his pistol.

The Python discharges.

Billy drops to the floor. As Margaret and Cameron rush to Billy, Ryan points the gun in their direction. Amanda, now with a free shot at Ryan, pulls the trigger, and the Python—along with a large portion of Ryan's hand—flies towards the patio door.

Outside, sirens fill the air.

Full Count

Extra Innings

Cameron enters Billy's hospital room to find Margaret, Reverend Timothy, and Rabbi Greene around his bed.

"We were just leaving for a quick bite to eat in the cafeteria." Before leaving, Margaret takes Cameron's hand. "You doing all right?"

"I'm fine," Cameron assures her.

"Don't guess I'll break four hundred this year," says Billy.

When Ryan pulled the trigger of the Colt Python, it launched a .357 caliber bullet at twenty-seven hundred feet per second. The bullet pierced the skin of Billy's right upper arm and splintered his humerus, and exited through the back of his arm. After three days of tests, the doctors have announced that no surgery is necessary, but that it will be at least a year before Billy can swing a bat.

"What's that?" Cameron asks, pointing to a stack of letters by the bed.

"Fan mail."

"I can help you answer it," Cameron says.

"First I want you to write an open letter to the press for me."

"What do you want it to say?"

"I love Cameron Lawrence."

"I don't think that's a good idea."

"I knew you wouldn't."

Six years later, there are four openly gay players in professional baseball, and all of them are present at Billy's press conference to announce his retirement.

Lee Edwards—who won a Pulitzer for his photograph of Ryan Rigsby's hand flying through the air as Margaret and Cameron rushed to Billy—snaps photos as Billy dumps two large duffel bags of letters on a table and begins his brief speech.

"These are the letters I've received over the past six years from high school athletes. Gay high school athletes." He takes a baseball from his jacket pocket. "This is a game," he says, holding up the baseball. "And these are lives," he says, passing his bullet-scarred arm over the pile of letters. "If I've left my mark on either one, I hope it's the latter."

After a long round of applause and several questions from the press, Billy and Cameron drive to the coast.

On board *Sam I Am II*, Cameron and Billy sit on the bow and drink gin and pink lemonade. By the end of their second cocktail, Amanda arrives carrying two bags of groceries. "Catch, Billy," comes a small voice from behind her.

"Impressive," says Billy, smiling as he snatches the ball from the clear summer sky.

About the Author

A former tennis instructor, securities broker, barge driver, and tree surgeon, Win Neagle now teaches in the English Department at Louisburg College where he chairs the Division of Humanities. He is an avid poker player and the head columnist for PokerLeagueManager.com. He lives in Raleigh with his wife, Rebecca, and their two dachshund puppies, Lola and Molly.

Neagle is also the author of *Smoke and Gravity*.

About the Cover

Acclaimed Raleigh, North Carolina artist Richard "Dick" Larsen provided the oil on canvas *Woman in Red Hat Getting Ready for Church* for the cover. Larsen spends his days in Wake Forest painting in his studio. On occasion you may find him—like a fine gentleman—holding the door for you at Burkenstock's, a local eatery and art gallery located in historic downtown Wake Forest.